RUE ST-DENIS

Rue St-Denis
Fantastic Tales

ANDRÉ CARPENTIER

Translated from the French
by Leonard W. Sugden

Ekstasis  Editions

Canadian Cataloguing in Publication Data

Carpentier, André
[Rue Saint-Denis. English]
Rue Saint-Denis

Translation of: Rue Saint-Denis.
ISBN 1-896860-64-8

I. Sugden, Leonard W. II. Title.
PS8555.A7618R8413 2001   C843'.54   C00-911394-0
PR3919.2.C234R8413 2001

© André Carpentier and Hurtubise HMH, 1986, 2001.
Translation © Leonard Sugden, 2001
Cover Art and Design: Miles Lowry

This book is a work of fiction. Names, characters, places and incidents are either the product of the author's imagination or are used fictionally. Any resemblance to actual events or locales or persons living or dead, is entirely coincidental. All rights reserved. No portion of this publication may be reproduced in any manner without written permission from author or publisher, except by a reviewer who wishes to quote brief passages for inclusion in a review.

The original French, *Rue Saint-Denis* was published by Les Editions Hurtubise HMH Ltèe, 1815, avenue De Lorimer, Montreal, Quebec H2K 3W6, in 1978.

Published in 2001 by:
Ekstasis Editions Canada Ltd.

Box 8474, Main Postal Outlet
Victoria, B.C. v8w 3s1

Box 571
Banff, Alberta t0l 0c0

The translation of *Rue Saint-Denis* has been done with the assistance of the Canada Council for the Arts Translation Program. *Rue Saint-Denis* has been published with the assistance of a grant from the Canada Council for the Arts and the Cultural Services Branch of British Columbia.

Contents

Introduction	7
Notes	16
Perrine Blanc's Seven Dreams and Reality	19
Magus Pichu Master of Magic	39
The Heaven-Sent World Map	50
Bi's Bell	57
Madam Corriveau's Chest	69
Casius Sahbid's Fatala	84
Victorine's Flower Shop	90
Ogda's Double	98
The Between-Time Bookshop	103
Chronology	123

INTRODUCTION

A writer's freedom seems to be inscribed in the chromosome of contradiction. This is why he is joyously lured by the unnameable, why he reveals the unthinkable or shuns the incontestable.

André Carpentier
Journal Of A Thousand Days

In 1978, André Carpentier was little known in literary circles. Notwithstanding, he had published, five years before, a first work, *Axel and Nicholas*, followed by *Mémoires d'Axel*, Roman-puzzle[1], received by critics at that time with doubtful enthusiasm. This first misadventure didn't deter him from pursuing a career in writing. Perhaps it even helped him to refine his aesthetic approach even if he did not alter his course. All the same, Carpentier preserved what was best in his puzzle-novel, that is to say, its baroque aspect which was transposed into a fantasy / fantastic form in his second novel, *L'aigle volera à travers le soleil*.[2] He next shed heavy textual excess by adopting, already in *Rue Saint-Denis*, a briefer form along with the aesthetics of fantastic writing. He was to maintain this latter double option from 1978 to 1988, sometimes enjoying the odd incursion into science-fiction, humour and crime stories, while still composing in a brief narrative style. Nor was he to deviate from his main path — the fantastic novel — which brought about another collection of stories, *Du pain des oiseaux*[3], and a series of collective works[4], which show Carpentier as a "defender of the short story," such as he himself defines this genre.

Before becoming an advocate of the brief style we know him for — having been its forerunner and even the one who gave impetus to the recent vogue in short story writing in Quebec — Carpentier went about creating his stories while carefully styling them in the great tradition of the Western fantastic mode. The reasons for his new orientation, between the first novel in 1973 and the two 1978 works, are obscure, unless we take into consideration the fact that, in the interim, he went on with his university studies in psychology and spent some time in Alsace, often reputed as the land of the fantastic. Frequenting this particular region might therefore have stimulated his taste for attempting to express the inexpressible.

With *Rue Saint-Denis*, there are three aspects of the text the reader should pay particular attention to: first of all, the thematic one, principally in so far as the fantastic is concerned, but also a series of related themes (the quest, the dream, the desire ...), which give such a particular texture to Carpentier's fantasies; next, the formal aspect, by this we mean the overlappings of discourse, the blending of voices, the manner of setting them out, of identifying them or of having them dissolve in a single crucible; in this respect, Carpentier then and there establishes his distinctiveness as a creator of fantastic tales. However, his greatest originality lies in touches of parody and stylistic features, that is to say, those that are truly micro-textual.

In Carpentier's work, a lover of the fantastic finds himself to be quite in his element. Everything is there, from great thematic sources (doubles, inexplicable appearances and disappearances, regressions in time, the animation of inanimate objects) to the subtle or large-scale presence of magic and maleficence. This all quite clearly fits in with the eminent system of symbols identified with the fantastic such as the already long tradition of this genre has bequeathed to us, one going back, broadly speaking, to the end of the 18th Century. With Carpentier, there are, therefore, signs of preromanticism (the terrifying gothic, for example) and of German romanticism, as André Belleau points out[5] (unless it be merely a question of a personal current of thought and sensibility), as much as what may be modern influences (the fantastic Latin American style, for example).

What binds all these influences together (if such be the case) is the way Carpentier manipulates his use of the fantastic. He constructs "études" or "variations" (in the musical sense of these terms) on his fantastic themes. Instead of limiting himself to a conventional or largely traditional treatment (one which maintains an atmosphere of doubt while seeking to inspire terror on the part of his protagonists), Carpentier prefers a modern vision of the fantastic which doesn't merely result in a superficial and too obvious a recording of modern urban settings. He chooses rather to root magic and maleficence in the very consciousness of his characters who are living, according to the precepts of the fantastic genre, in a world which is quite familiar even though pervaded by literally unbelievable but fiercely assertive phenomena. The difference of Carpentier's approach from a time-honoured tradition lies in the fact that, in his fiction, his characters, far from being perpetually surprised (as is so often the case) by the appearance of the impossible, discover that they call forth what is strange and magical in all their wishes and that this fits in closely with an objectification of their most intimate desires (be they healthy or unhealthy).

This does not identify these texts with what has been styled as "the marvellous" since, for such an aesthetic to be in practice, the world invoked must be, from the outset, mythical or presented as in a fairy tale. With Carpentier, it is never a question of "once upon a time ... " but merely the portrayal of a reality in the pure tradition of a realist narrative (elements which are, moreover, essential to the fantastic genre). And so, from this point of view, the difference between a traditionally fantastic tale and a modern one is only very slight. It is enough for the game of the fantastic to be played on the protagonist (by breathing into his discourse necessary indications of his resistance to occult events), while, at the same time, having the unbelievable gradually assert itself, without there being, in the end, even the slightest doubt as to its presence.

Since Lovecraft, this practice is quite common, but it is above all with writers such as Jorge Luis Borges, Julio Cortazar or Gabriel Garcia Marquez that the contemporary practice of inserting magic into fictional reality has been established as a dominant code, although the German romantics, and also Nerval, worked over their imaginary worlds in this way. It appears that this style of writing is one of the world's oldest (one has but to think of the presence of the Gods in the imaginings of the ancient Greeks and of the fabulous things contained in Roman writings, in those of the Middle Ages, the Renaissance and even during the Age of Enlightenment); moreover, it has become, in the form indicated by the expression "magic realism," one of the major currents in post modern literature. It is with this latter important trend, which is both modern and timeworn, that Carpentier's work is incontestably related, as are those of a goodly number of Quebec writers.

Carpentier is, in any case, original in the way he mingles his characters' voices and includes his own. The composition and style of *Rue Saint-Denis* are permeated with an obsessional concern for investigating the real, for questioning the advent of the inexplicable, even when the character discovers that it is out of a profound desire for a change of scenery and for personal distinction that arises, first in his own reality, then in reality in general, this apparition of the improbable and the unbelievable. The same pattern repeats itself in the case of Perrine Blanc or of Luc/Lucien Guindon: both (or is it all three?) prefer to take their desires and dreams for reality; from the former to the latter, there is only one step, a step cheerfully traversed by fiction. Magic (or maleficence) asserts itself through the powers of a (fourfold) will, as is the case for the two vengeful protagonists in the Magus Pichu's shop, but this backfires on the unobservant Magician. On the other hand, 'misfortune' strikes unannounced those who frequent the business known by the impressive name "the Treasure Seeker" or those surrounding Victorine's Flower Shop. It arises still more unexpectedly in "The Heaven-sent World Map" and in "Casius Sahbid's Fatala." Heaven literally falls upon the heads of these poor people and their reactions of fear and marvelling is all the more instructive. Each short story, in this regard, offers a particular type of discourse, while at the same time placing in the immediate concerns of the (narrators) and characters a similar type of event: the apparition of the occult.

Among the non-fantastic interests serving to support the fantastic side of Carpentier's writings, one element of content stands out quite clearly in *Rue Saint-Denis* — business and money appear to be keynotes of evil, but with one exception: the book business. The merchants of pseudo-sciences (parapsychology, occultism, black magic) or the dealers in antique treasures sell evil by exploiting the gullibility of people, whereas the book salesman, through his more noble business, transmits knowledge. The former are decked out in names that are relatively weird, satirical or paradoxical: with Mathieu Levant, named the Prince of Sleep, in "The Seven Dreams" 'levant' suggests 'rising' while his client is lying (*couchant*) asleep before him; the Magus Pichu, Master of Magic, in the so-named short story, is actually master of very little; the Treasure Seeker, in "Madam Corriveau's Chest" has a name which parodies the poor title of Quebec's first novel, *L'Influence d'un livre* (1837), readapted by the abbé Henri-Raymond Casgrain. All of these are relatively speaking, princes of darkness who cause the death or disappearance of others by seeking to amass 'filthy lucre.' They are all in search of some fairly concrete possession; Bi, in "Bi's Bell" is torn to pieces for having been too ardent in his wish to gain a fortune by defying the mysteries of a haunted house.

On the other hand, a quest for knowledge is given high value. The bookstore salesman and writer-protagonist in "The Beyond-Time Bookshop" seem to be indifferent to the possessions of this world, having rather the appearance of quite affable artists. There is, then, here, if you wish, an extremely positive representation of literary things in a social context, having little to do with the fantastic, but which gains all its importance from the fact that this thematic current involves a fantastic treatment. Why would this style have been adopted? The fact of the matter is that it was probably unconscious, in the same way as Perrine Blanc is shown to have a penchant for seeking her own destruction/rebirth. There is then, in this dialectic of having and knowing, of the use of reason and the exploitation of human gullibility, a fundamental question that the fantastic, more than any other genre, is suited to explore. Introducing within the narrative, at various moments, a sort of discussion of the improbable, a fantastic tale conceals within its very depths one of the essential elements in the functioning of the human mind: the act of questioning. Indeed, to a certain extent, any text whatever puts the real into question; however, in the case of the fantastic, the investigation is quite fundamental: it deals with the profound nature of things and their character which is, as it were, sacred, secret, undefinable and indescribable. In this way, a fantastic narrative can also be disappointing because it cannot produce an absolute answer to things and must be satisfied with partially removing the shroud from certain strange phenomena fascinating to the human spirit. With Carpentier, the paradoxical dualism of having and knowing operates under the aegis of power, a power capable, at least in fiction, of transforming the real and the imaginary that the unconscious world of desires and dreams brings into being, be it for the better or for worse. Between knowing and having, the question of power sways back and forth, a power tilting sometimes towards good and sometimes the other way.

There is, then, in the fantastic mode used by Carpentier, quite a particular commitment to "reality." This arises from an ideology and axiology whose implications are highly complex and would really require an entire volume to explore since, in order to understand the phenomenon of attitudes and values contained in these texts, a good deal of space would have to be given to their content and means of expression. However, Carpentier's works also reflect an intense stylistic effort which reveals the crafting of the text, the work of a watchmaker shown to be highly worth while in a deeper analysis. This writing seems to contain, maintain and even to provoke a sort of outlook or view upon the world. When, for example, Luc Guindon prepares to skip from one century to another, moving from the Montreal of 1978 to that of 1878, the narrator spends a good deal of effort in creating an effect of artistic blurring, fading or narrative scrambling. This takes the form of a sort of disincarnation, a suppressed sense of reality insofar as what is being portrayed. The vocabulary expands with words or ethereal metaphors such as 'mystery,' 'shadow,' 'shade,' 'souls,' 'nightbird,' 'confuse,' 'half-light,' 'light and shade ... ' Everything converges in producing the impression of a "sort of gigantic (textual) scene showing the details of a flight beyond the darkness of the ages." These stylistic traits contain the principal design of the fantastic style — and of the entire style — of *Rue Saint-Denis*. The question of the power of words is therefore linked to the power of the characters' desires, secret desires seeking to become reality. One could go on and on with this aspect of our analysis.

Finally, the ultimate image or system of images marking Carpentier's prose could be taken to be a sort of labyrinth: a psychological labyrinth, a spacio-temporal labyrinth and a scriptural (discursive and stylistic) one. "You are moving forward, towards the unknown (...). And these fears grow less as repose guides you along through this maze made up of your fantasies and dreams ... " so says the pernicious but observant Prince of Sleep. The Magus Pichu pays with his life for the fact that he had not properly explored the maze of his powers; Bi dies in a booby-trapped labyrinthian house; the Treasure Seeker's victim must pass through a space far from simple, even though secret, in order to satisfy the magician's demands; the detective in "Casius Sahbid's Fatala," strolling through the maze of a port city, also pays with his life for his lack of foresight at the close of this crime story (he is choked by a cable, an Ariadne's anti-thread, much like the cord that kills Bi); as for the wanderings of Luc / Lucien, it is based both on a narcissistic blueprint (a spectacular voyage towards the self), and a "Thesean" one, in the sense that Luc, moving about within his own genetic and temporal labyrinth, is unconsciously in search of a Minotaur who is no one other than himself. And so we once again discover that "chromosome of contradiction" that Carpentier refers to in his *Journal of a thousand days.*

All of these figures, whether they be personified, presented in space, in time or otherwise, advance along this path which has the advantage of never being simple. They, in fact, allow the author great liberties and give Carpentier's fantastic tales the visage he is now known for for some ten years, that is to say, a protean one. The nine paths followed in this collection show quite well the qualities and progression of such an undertaking; from the maleficent charlatanism of a Mathieu Levant, embroiled as he is in commercial affairs, to the magic and paradoxical realisations of the intimate desires of Perrine Blanc and Luc / Lucien Guindon, the reader of Carpentier's phantasmagorical dramas, is witness to lethal and euphoric games of apparitions, disappearances and manipulations.

The re-edition of *Rue Saint-Denis* allows once again this occult fictional knowledge to be renewed in the form of a book that a bookshop of our time has found in a shop of some other time — still quite recent but already rather far removed. We have now but to accept being manipulated, while we read, and to go along with the game of the improbable.

Michel Lord

NOTES

1. André Carpentier, *Axel et Nicholas* followed by *Mémoires d'Axel*. Roman-puzzle, Montréal, éditions du Jour, 1973, 177 p.

2. Ibid., *L'aigle volera à travers le soleil*, roman. Montréal, Hurtubise HMH, 1978, 176 p.

3. Ibid., *Du pain des oiseaux*, récits. Préface by André Belleau. Montréal, VLB editor, 1982, 149 p.

4. André Carpentier first prepared, along with Marie José Thériault, the special number of *La Nouvelle Barre du Jour* (no. 89, April 1980) on the fantastic, then, alone, *Dix contes et nouvelles fantastiques*. Montréal, Quinze, 1983, 204 p. Next appeared the collections of short stories on science-fiction, humour, love and adventure.

5. André Belleau, "André Carpentier et le discours littéraire fantastique." *Imagine* ... , no. 22 (vol. V, no. 5, June, 1984) p. 31-35.

I shudder as I tell it.

Virgil

André Carpentier

PERRINE BLANC'S SEVEN DREAMS AND REALITY

Dreams are the aquarium of the night.
Victor Hugo

Perrine Blanc was born on the first of October, 1948 in the Saint-Louis district, offspring of Rose Blanc, formerly Cormier, and Iréné Blanc, a tailor in leather by trade who conceived this first daughter during a snowstorm holiday the day after the first of the year 1948.

Today Perrine is thirty years old. She is still living in the district of her earliest years above Rodolphe Brisebois' after hour store, formerly Brisebois' Corner Restaurant. She is living with Mathieu Levant, known as "the Prince of Sleep," who earns a comfortable living as an oneirologist at the Centre for Psychic Consultation on rue Saint-Denis. There he assists his patients principally through hypnosis in an effort to expose the heavy secrets of their dreams. His method being halfway between psychoanalysis and charlatanism, he only reveals to patients what they actually want to hear themselves.

Rue St-Denis

Perrine is well acquainted with this manoeuvre, too well, in any case, to have been fooled up to now and, although her own mental balance is rather precarious, she has always refused any kind of intervention on the part of the Prince, preferring complete uncertainty to his approximations.

Now, today Perrine is thirty and the idea of it is quite unbearable for her! Considering the tempo of her life and her frequent nervous upsets, she is no longer sure whether she is arriving or leaving, whether she is closer to the blast than to its impact. This produces within her as well an unpleasant pressure somewhere between the heart and the stomach, a millstone, an unknown corrosive lump weighing down on her abdomen and eating away at her insides. Besides this, for some weeks, her nights are flooded with nightmares and her days, with obsessions, anguish and torment.

Her hands are given more and more to trembling; she feels cold and weeps as well without always knowing why.

Thus far, with the hope of rectifying her condition, she has first of all taken lengthy trips to Florida, but she found herself surrounded by so many Quebeckers there that she felt there was no real change of scenery at all. Next, it was yoga, judo and jazz ballet. But, on each occasion, amorous squabbles would arise and destroy the harmony of the groups she had become attached to. For Perrine is beautiful. Very beautiful! too beautiful, in her own opinion, and so very desirable ...

Finally, she took to sedatives; but, as it is quite understandable, this merely pushed her even further towards the brink. And so, completely distraught, she imagined she had no other solution than to confide in the dream breaker, the Prince of the Unsoundable Depths and of Sleep.

Now, Mathieu Levant, the so-called Prince, had been waiting for this occasion for some time. He had even prepared for it quite meticulously. Moreover, so as to avoid any professional relationship between Perrine and himself and in order to create a more intimate and everyday atmosphere rather than holding his seances at the Centre for Psychic Consultation, one Sunday evening, he decided to work right in his companion's bedroom.

First, he made her undress, then lie out on the copper bed that Perrine's own mother had repurchased from the Brisebois family at the death of Perrine's mother, a bed Perrine always considered to be a sort of fetish.

Strangely enough, she felt quite calm, as though her own destiny no longer depended only upon herself, as though her existence was no longer merely her own.

"I'm asking you to have confidence in me. You have to trust me," the Prince kept saying. "You scoff at me claiming that I only tell patients what they already want to hear; but you're only half right, for what they want to hear is exactly the thing that's troubling them. However, they are not able to give expression to it all because they only perceive it ambiguously or refuse to really have any faith. Now, you, you know what you want to hear. And you'll hear it, coming from your own thoughts. You want the truth and you'll have it. Starting from this moment you're tuned in to yourself. Your dreams are the reflection of your own deepest preoccupations, of your most persistent anguish. During the hours that follow, you're going to have seven dreams ... "

"Seven dreams!" she exclaimed. "You want me to have seven dreams!"

Perrine recognized here the main thrust the Centre for Psychic Consultation's advertising campaign featuring a four part programme: *the summoning of dreams:* a form of concentration and general relaxation with, as its main objective, calming anxious people and restoring them to sleep, *the very basis of psychic equilibrium* (eight seances); *enlightened sleep*: the most advanced form of relaxation and concentration strongly related to yoga and intended principally for curing anguish (eight seances); *mastering dreams*: an exercise in introducing volition into the field of dreams (seven seances); *the seven dreams*: the project's final step: in a state of hypnotic trance, the patient is lead to retrace the 'seven key images' which represent at one and the same time the origins and development of his or her anguish (seven seances). The complete cure is composed of thirty seances in progressive order, each lasting an hour. The fee is comes to $20.00 per seance and, if the client pays in advance, the total price is $500.00.

Up until then, a quarter of his patients had reached the stage of "seven dreams" and all those who had attained this level had come to the seventh seance, the seventh dream! And furthermore, the latter were named "self-awareness recoveries" in the same poor style as others had been called "miraculous recoveries"!

From the beginning, that is to say for more than eighteen months, only a few complaints had arrived at the consumers' protection agencies, and only two had come to the small claims court, both of them failing in their claims. Moreover, and this is worth noting, none of the complaints had come from the small faithful group of "self-awareness recoveries."

But none of this was really enough to reassure Perrine. She could remember only too well the appearance of these "self-aware" cases who grew skinnier and more sickly from week to week, appearing to go visibly downhill from one seance to the other. She spoke to the Prince about this.

"You're judging with your eyes, Perrine, rather than with your heart. Our friends who have reached the stage of the seven dreams have attained a state of bliss. You no longer see them in offices and factories pretending they're living while they watch death make greater and greater inroads within their metabolism.. They have over-come fears which were senseless, ridiculous and unjustified. They are 'aware.'"

Her hand was trembling, her eyes were darting about and drops of sweat stood out on her forehead. Then, suddenly, she held her mouth so tight it was as though her lips were about to burst. Once again, she was filled with anguish.

"You're afraid of death, Perrine. Don't feel like that, for it's only a stage, a step, a deliverance ... You're afraid to die much in the same way a foetus fears being born. You dread the unknown, you're afraid of what's to come."

Suddenly the fears of the last few moments were transformed into a sort of richness as though she were a long silent glass corridor in the midst of a storm.

"However, you are advancing towards this unknown; sleep is leading you that way. You are moving forward, dream after dream, towards the origin of your fears. And these fears grow less as repose guides you along through this maze made up of your fantasies and dreams.."

She didn't resist for long. At first, feeling she was wandering through the desert, then, as if, reclining in a hammock, she were being lulled by warm breeze, she allowed herself to slide into the depths of sleep ... searching out her first dream.

The first dream

The wooden counter has a lemony odour. The overnight cleaning unit must have sprayed it with *Pledge* so that the bank manager might surmise, from the smell, that dust must have completely vanished from his silver and paper universe.

During the week, there were no more than two cashiers in this shoddy little branch of the business centre, even though, since the sudden departure of one of them four days before, one was enough to do the job.

The man, crowned with an astonishingly large dome, who was explaining to Perrine the rudiments of the trade, was the branch's accountant. Besides, the simple fact that he had been placed there as though in a sort of train siding, demonstrated the rather low esteem his superiors held him in. This was probably due to his physical deformity.

"Our branch isn't really very mechanized, our cashiers have to fill out this sheet, marking credits on the left and debits on the right."

The poor fellow exhaled a very bad breath. He also seemed to be examining his new cashier as an eagle might his prey. Screwing his face up in a sombre and rather sardonic smile, he went on:

"When a customer *comes* to deposit money, you enter it on the left, and when he *takes* out money, you *enter it* on the right."

What was this fellow thinking of punctuating his speech with such coarse subliminal intimations, along with gazing at her breasts rather than into her eyes!

"Look, here's your first "customer"."

The final image in this dream came with a shock, just as it did when it actually happened, a little more than two years ago. The man before her was handsome, proud and enigmatic. Strangely enough, it was as though she had been waiting for him for a long time without realizing it. As though she had come all this way to work in this bank unconscious of the fact she was hoping to meet him.

At first sight, she recoiled as though standing before a magnificent picture viewed from too close, then a wave of warmth rose between her thighs ...

"Mathieu, I dreamed of you," she said to him, as she awakened.

A few warm tears stole across her cold temple, leaving a salty trail from the corner of her eye to her hairline. But she remained silent, thus avoiding telling him how much she had wanted him for the first weeks, then subsequently loved him, until they got together to set up the Centre for Psychic Consultation, then, began a life together that grew more and more shaky, more and more devoted to business and money problems. She also avoided admitting how, ever since, she had buried all of this love under tons of other stray memories, probably since business relations had come to take precedence over romantic ones, first of all in Mathieu's mind, but, in time and due to circumstances, in her own as well!

Along with this, she had the feeling of having fished back her own boot tossed into the water a few months before in a sudden impulse. However, the Prince went right on, not giving her any time to think ...

"Do you still have confidence in me? Do you still want to go on with this unswerving process your mind is following on the path towards self-awareness?"

Bowed down with weariness, Perrine nodded her head. So he immediately had her plunge once again deep inside herself on the trail of a second dream. "Any one at all," the Prince reflected, "provided it guides her as rapidly and efficiently as possible towards wiping out the sources of her misery ... and of mine!"

Rue St-Denis

The second dream

That day, Perrine wore her hair smoothed and tied in a bun at the back of her head. This was probably so as to be better able slip into her uniform for it is well known, hostesses at Man and his World, as is the case elsewhere, always wear a uniform.

In the summer of 1968 Perrine was twenty-one. At that very moment, she was strolling through the heavy and exuberant Saturday crowd. Earlier, before arriving at the site, she had gone to smoke a joint with the girls behind the municipal pool on Saint Helen's Island.

She was hot, very hot. Her very pale Senneterre crêpe uniform was sticking to her skin. Her belt with its metal buckle bearing the replica of Man and his World dug into her every time she took a step forward. Her mao collar on her uniform, stiffened with sweat, was reddening the skin on her neck while her white, pale blue and navy beret made her look like a life buoy on a wavy sea.

A young guard was walking with her, he too all crumpled and muggy in his grey uniform. His white short-sleeved shirt was sticking to his ribs and shoulder blades. He too was hot and, beneath his cap, having his hair so short and moustache shaven off, he found it unbearable. He felt as though his true personality had been exchanged, even though it was only temporarily, for another one more suitable for letting him spend another year at university.

Every three steps, Perrine, highly attracted to the guard's mouth and long legs, allowed her sticky arm to brush against the young man's even more sticky one. She would have liked to lick the sweat on his white arm, while these caresses didn't require him to show any boldness himself. She would also have liked to fondle his neck, mingle her sweat with his own …

She was shivering under the blazing sun, watching his long fingers while imagining them and almost feeling them on her flesh.

Upon awakening, still quivering as she had in her dream, she didn't understand too well the significance of this fantasy, of these feelings. She only felt a bit more weary.

She reflected on all this as if it were some catastrophic image, one neither fitting in with dreams nor with reality. She also noticed that she didn't even remember the name of the shy young man whom she had led on and who had made love with her most awkwardly one August night during that same summer, under the Concord Bridge ... .

With her hands hugging her elbows quite tightly, she withdrew into herself, in search of a bit of warmth.

"Have you followed your progress," the Prince asked.

She hadn't followed any. Besides this, strangely enough, she wasn't making any effort to analyse herself. Here I am, floating free on a raft, she thought, rudderless and not understanding at all the sinister role the Prince is playing in this business; she merely let herself drift off ... into sleep ... and into another dream.

The third dream

In the Diamond Taxi *dispatch room*, eight women, most of them being around fifty, were answering their customers' calls while munching chocolate and smoking menthol cigarettes. Facing them, four men, all of them veterans of the last war, were sending the same messages over private lines to the drivers stationed at numerous taxi stands in the city. Farther on, three men, younger than the others and also disabled, though these were victims of taxi accidents, were sending some of these messages to radio taxis. And at the very back, as though perched on his throne, the dispatcher sorted the calls received by the eight women and distributed them, according to district, to the seven men in front of him.

In the midst of this gigantic clamour that filled the room, the supervisor and his assistant followed each other about, watching over discipline and answering customers' questions passed on by the eight women and the drivers' inquiries conveyed by the seven men. Then, still one after the other, following the direction indicated by the worn flooring, they would walk back and lock themselves away in the small glassed in office at the back.

Perrine was working in this dusty office situated on the first floor of a relatively new building on Prince Arthur Street since mid-June, or, in other words, since the end of classes. It was her first summer job. She was sixteen.

Up until then, she had always worked "on the women's side," as it was called in that pokey office, chewing gum, smoking cigarette after cigarette to pass the time and continually glancing towards "the men's side." Her interest was above all for the dispatcher, a tall fellow with smooth black hair, slim shoulders and an intelligent look. A bit proud, a bit shy.

Besides this, several times over, just as a joke, she had sent him calls from fake customers, phony calls appearing less and less obscure, such as:

"Madam Elvire Love.

6 Lovers' Lane."

Now, that morning, probably drawn by Perrine's still youthful beauty, the supervisor had offered to have her come to "the men's side," to work, in particular, on radio messages.

Up until then, only one woman had been moved to this job, and the experience had proven to be disastrous. Several drivers, in point of fact, lost in the crowd, had immediately begun shouting taunts over the airwaves that were wild enough to make even the toughest and most experienced in the trade blush.

Upon placing the earphones on her head, Perrine had no idea what was coming next, for no one had warned her of the fate of the first of her kind.

At first, a few messages fell into the little box before her with a rhythmic rustling. She picked one of them up at random and announced:

"Saint-Denis and Jean-Talon."

Then and there, it was mayhem! Four or five drivers, cruising around in that part of the town, all tried to identify themselves at one and the same time by quite literally shouting out their respective numbers. The trick was to give the fare to the first driver to identify himself. Perrine tried to catch a number on the fly.

"You're eleven hundred and forty?"

She had taken the bait! Now there was chaos — an outburst of crazy remarks, crude comments, lewd banter and vulgarities of every kind! Immediately, Perrine found herself in a state of panic.Everyone around her saw her redden and look thoroughly mortified.

"Send out another message!" said the supervisor who also served as her instructor in these circumstances ... this helping him to edge a bit closer! But at the same time that he was endeavouring to assist her, he, like the others around them, couldn't help giving way to a heavy crude laugh.

Perrine then grabbed hold of another message in the little box and came out again, quite loud and spontaneously with:

"Lovers' Lane!"

Again there was a chain reaction! And this time, Perrine's numbness was accompanied by a sovereign desire to go home and take a bath, to wipe everything out — earphones, supervisor and the dispatcher, that lousy traitor!

This time, her awakening was more turbulent, more tormented. Furthermore, it took her a bit of time to come back around. For a few seconds even, she didn't really know where she was, whether in space or time. These dreams, one after the other, were really beginning to get to her, to prevent her from returning to the present.

It was only when she perceived the shadow of the Prince of Sleep above her that she began to come back to reality.

"And so?" he said.

Then, she spoke to him briefly, oh! very briefly, about these three dreams that were like a series of memories of sexual fantasies rising out of her feminine past, watching out not to refer to this strange intimate sensation which she had, moreover, completely suppressed like so many other things in her past — that adolescent need to purify her soul or mind by ridding her body of sweat and other daily hints of dirt ...

But he really gave her very little time to relax, having her descend right away again into the world of dreams.

He thought she was pretty simple not to have understood his ploy.

The fourth dream

The family bathroom had doubtlessly never been so empty. Nor so "unfamily" in tone. Whereas, a few days before, there was no way in the morning to use the wash basin and mirror for more than five minutes, that day Perrine had all the time in the world to wash, put on make up, do her hair, even to get dressed. She carried out each of these tasks infinitely slowly, accentuating her new solitude and giving weight to each of her actions with abundant ceremony, one given to remembering, or rather, one searching for memories.

Perrine was eight years old that day and she did her eyes clumsily, coating them with make up and mascara. She powdered her cheeks and did her hair up like Doris Day. She was trying to bring out her womanliness, probably in an attempt to understand the sudden and unexpected loss of her father, but also of her two younger sisters, in an automobile accident.

And just when she was putting on her black dress trimmed in white lace at the wrists and neck, she could see her mother once again, absolutely wild, arriving to announce the tragic accident in this very same bathroom where she was playing with make-up and getting herself up as a 'madame.'

Besides this, for the three last days she had kept on covering herself with make-up so as to hide away from the growing sorrow for which she could find neither a remedy nor an escape.

In a few minutes, they were coming to pick her up for the final ceremony, the burial. And she was to be alone with family and friends, for her mother, having suffered a severe nervous shock the day after the accident, had had to be hospitalized.

Perrine was to be wife and mother during this ceremony. However, and this is what was eating away at her, she had very limited memories of this great traveller they had so often waited for and wanted home. She was aware that hidden within her she guarded images of happier days, fatherly caresses, surprises and presents, stories before bedtime and family outings. But of these, none of them would return to the surface. She even caught herself — and believed she felt wretched over it — searching for her father's face in her memories. She was no longer able to see her father's features nor hear his melodious deep voice.

This too she had suppressed in her early childhood. She wept bitterly, rubbing her funny looking eyes with her knuckles.

When she awakened, this time completely exhausted, she felt quite crushed. Or it could be rather said that something had tried to crush her but she had just managed to escape. She felt she was in a vice even though she wasn't being crunched any more. She was oppressed, bearing a deep sorrow in her tiny child's hands.

She felt as well that she was blameless, but was constrained by sorrow and feelings of guilt and remorse. At the same time, she experienced a strange pressure deep in her stomach, much as she had in her dream, as though a heavy warm mass had long weighed against her abdomen and that this mass had just left her. "It was like a vice even though she was no longer being squelched ..."

However, she didn't have time to establish a link between dreams and reality, for the Prince, both for selfish motives as well as in order to finish with this awkward ineffectual partner, subjected her to the fifth dream while showing no pity or consideration.

The fifth dream

First of all, there was a long streak of lightning and a prolonged clap of thunder in the open sky above the orchard. Perrine wedged herself between her grandfather's legs, her little arms being just enough to encircle fat Laureat's hip. Everyone around her started to laugh.

"Are you afraid, Perrine?" her father asked.

"Not afraid," she answered proudly, the end of her nose scarcely protruding from Laureat's ample trousers.

But a second rumble of thunder was enough to have her dive back beneath her grandfather's protective legs.

This time, hoping that the small group would have the time to arrive home before the storm, her father seized Perrine by the wrist and marched headlong towards the old white house belonging to Laureat and Marie.

They rushed along full tilt, with the father ahead of them, pulling Perrine who, digging her heals into the ground, attempted to slow them up. Next came Laureat, more aged and weary than ever, (all the more so since his only son had just refused to once again take care of the family orchard), and then, her mother, Rose, altogether quite disappointed at not being able to come and live in the country; and, close by her, stretching out the clustered band, their grandmother, Marie, looking thoughtful, sad and downcast as well.

Suddenly, with a more vigorous jolt, Perrine succeeded in escaping her father's vice-like grip and ran over to swing from one of the lower branch of an apple tree seemingly more twisted than the others.

Her father first of all began to shout, but the wind lessened the effects of his anger; then it was her mother who attempted to reason with her, conjuring up colds, flue and even pneumonia! However, nothing worked. Perrine didn't want to leave her beloved orchard that her father had just turned down. She was furious with him as was her mother for they had heard Laureat talk of selling! Even Marie, this grandmother whom she so much adored, couldn't manage, through her gentle promises of candy and cake, to convince her to come home. But suddenly from behind the two women rose Laureat's low warm voice:

"That tree is yours, Perrine. I'm giving it to you, since you are much like it. It will always belong to you, whatever happens."

That strange sensation, so close to her for so many years and that she felt at that instant, filled her with both sadness and joy. However, Perrine still didn't want to go home. She then wanted to stay more than ever in her garden and in her tree!

All day long she held out against the thunder, the lightning, the rain and the damp and cold of late fall.

After that day, Perrine never saw her tree again. But she went on loving it, at first with sadness and pain then, as an adolescent, she became bitter and this was followed by feeling rather listless about it ever since — a hidden dull feeling that she was still encumbered with during the brief moment of wakefulness the Prince now allowed her. She scarcely had the time to experience this, along with a deep fatigue, a sort of visceral exhaustion, before again being immersed in another dream.

She hardly had time as well to reflect that grandmother Brisebois' bed, that her body was still bound to was to serve as a bed for display, a bed to lend her support in her final moments ...

Then the Prince understood, for his part, that she had now reached the fatal step in breaking away and that the Centre for Psychic Consultation was henceforth to belong to himself alone.

The sixth dream

Perrine was one year old. In fact, she was one on that very day sitting in an oval basin that was lilac or pink in tone, she waved her arms about splashing the entire kitchen including her mother who was bellowing and darting about all over the place, but in a maternal and adult way.

Perrine had a tiny red mark between her thumb and index finger which she was continuously concerned with, a small burn that she kept waving about, plunging into the water and sucking.

Earlier, at dessert, wanting to monopolize all the light, she had grabbed at the one candle on her birthday cake. The wax had run onto her hand, burning her slightly.

Her mother, Rose, was excited and probably exhausted from her day and the preparations for the little birthday party the maternal and paternal grandparents had been present at. However, while struggling against her fatigue, she showed infinite tenderness, as though her role was to love for two people rather than just herself! As though a father's love was only a matter of obligation and moral conduct! But Perrine couldn't be absolutely certain of this. She only knew that it had taken many years before he ever spoke to her of love, and accepted it between Rose and himself.

Perrine was now nicely propped beside her mother in the old bed of grandmother Brisebois who had died less than two years before. She was looking for all the physical and human warmth she could find.

She was also feeling quite dissatisfied, as though her need for love had remained unappeased throughout her life. This persistent feeling distressed her as she sank into total exhaustion. What was more, she no longer had the strength to lift an eyelid nor even the desire to awaken. She wanted not to waken at all.

Rue St-Denis

The Prince knew this and had her hurriedly sink into the depths of her last dream, one regarding her unavoidable death, one concerned with the past giving birth to the present. The revelation that will never penetrate the consolidated veil of collective ignorance ...

The seventh dream

The room was very dark. Since morning, the Venetian blinds and velvet drapes had been closed. The small Victorian-style bedside lamp covered with a printed silk sash gave but an orangy glow to this decor which was both sober and tinged with memories and the traces of time.

Outside, the sun glistened on the snow and flashed in tiny luminous specks as though it were toasting this New Year's Day. In the streets, people were going and coming, shaking hands and shouting good wishes to one another above the staccato rumblings of the local plough. Others were strolling about with heads down, alone, even quite isolated or simply unhappy. The stirring of knees and insteps "as slim as De Kuyper bottles" showed that some were already set to do some jigging.

Periodically, children from the district or holiday revellers, looking for *Cokes, Seven-up*, chips or peanuts came along to crowd against the door of Brisebois' Corner Restaurant. They were astonished that the business was closed on New Year's Day, for it was known that Brisebois' was virtually never closed. However, what people in the district didn't know was that grandmother Brisebois, who was observing her seventieth year on that New year's Day in 1948, was also dying.

Her children were marshalled around the old woman: her

daughter, Eva, the eldest, and her husband, a prominent lawyer; Céline along with her husband, a welder at Vickers: and Rodolph, her youngest darling, a bachelor who worked in the family restaurant since the father's death twenty-two years before.

Close to the bed stood Fabien Ménard, the family doctor who had brought the three children into the world and who was almost as old as grandmother Brisebois. He had retired four years before, but the mother wouldn't have anyone else at her bedside; it was said he had been her lover during the thirties, after the father's death.

"Tell me the truth, Fabien," she said in a faint voice.

"Listen, Emma ... you're seventy years old," he said, his eyes filled with tears, "and you're very tired. Your organism is worn out ... "

"Will it be today?"

"I don't know."

"On my birthday! New Year's Day! So, let everybody celebrate ... "

"But I didn't say ... "

"Keep quiet, I know. I can feel it ... My children, come close so that I can talk to you ... "

The children protested but, as she went on talking any way in a very soft voice, they had to gather around her.

"As for you, Eva, your husband has money and I've left you less than the others. Merely some small souvenirs. I know that if you cherish them, you will have understood what I have done. As for you, Céline, I leave you the house in the country. You need it, you. your wife and your children. Besides, I'm leaving it to them so you won't sell it and buy an automobile ... And you, Rodolph ... Rodolph Brisebois, how I dreamed about you before having you!

— dreamed of having a son called Rodolph, like Rodolph Valentino! Oh! your father never went along with this ... Rodolph, your father's restaurant is now yours, along with the house. You need it more than the others do. I want you to keep it, Rodolph ... "

Emma-Perrine, then, in the depths of her dream felt herself die twice over. Once under the hard self-satisfied gaze of Mathieu Levant, the Prince of Sleep, and another time, in the same bed, surrounded by her weeping children while, on the second floor, a young couple were making love several times a day, the young woman, named Rose, with the secret wish to have a child and the man, Iréné Blanc, merely out of natural desire.

However, along with this feeling of a double death, one natural and the other beyond-the-natural, Emma-Perrine also had the feeling of a double survival ... a double breath of life which let her move from Emma to Perrine and from Perrine to ...

André Carpentier

Magus Pichu Master of Magic

You never find a dove in a crow's nest.
Popular Saying

The man, dressed in white and sweating profusely in the heavy August humidity, ordered a beer even before sitting down. Then, he let himself slump into an uncomfortable white metal chair while consulting an old watch fixed to his jacket by a tarnished silver chain. It was only five o'clock — he still had two hours to wait, two hours that would seem all the longer since he was so given to perspiring. Not to mention that waiting for so serious an event as what was to occur around seven o'clock made him even more tense and anxious.

If only his brother, Janvier, could be not too late for once and come even a bit earlier to keep him company on this rue Saint-Denis terrace where the sun dispelled the wind and the air was heavier than a watered down martini ...

Alexis Duguay, born at l'Anse-à-Beaufils and living in Montreal for more than thirty-five years, had been waiting for his brother, Janvier, nearly an hour when suddenly he saw Janvier's white 1958 Monarch at the corner of Ontario Street. He saw him cautiously parking his collector's item car in between two BMW's of the same colour, which caused him to reflect that rue Saint-

Denis was no longer what it had been; the freaks had definitely given way to another class of young people, more privileged and more respectable, mixing joints with their aperitifs and often wearing pressed jeans; the shabby cafés were slowly being turned into goofy glittery bars; the rundown shops had been completely done over in shape and design; the life's blood of the strip had been transfused from Crescent Street. Yes, Saint-Denis was becoming a sort of Crescent Street of the east.

Watching Janvier cross the street like some bold toreador, Alexis noticed he was carrying a small package under his arm. When his brother reached the terrace, Alexis wanted to know if it had something to do with the doll that ... But Janvier cut him short, for he realized his brother had been drinking while he waited even though it had been agreed the night before that he was to keep away from it ... .

"Come on," Alexis reassured him, "I only had two beers, one for each leg ... "

Within a few seconds, the two brothers confronted each other like two young cocks, something they obviously hadn't been for some time. This quite naturally drew the attention of the bored drinkers at surrounding tables. Alexis gave him a last dig:

"And you're crazy enough to have gotten dressed the same as me!"

However, as he said this, he knew very well that both being decked out in similar and fairly bold white suits with smooth wide cuffs wouldn't prevent them from walking virtually unobserved down a street like Saint-Denis. Much to the contrary.

And when, to quash Alexis' penchant for drinking, they decided to leave the terrace and go for a stroll while waiting for the big event, no one paid any attention to them, that is to say, other than the manager who, with a simple peek at the waitress, checked to see that the two men had paid; there was also, a young blond in a corner, hiding behind dark glasses, who was rather tentatively on the look out for some well fed well dressed customer. If her glance betrayed an interest in the two men, their *nouveau riche* appearance seemed to suggest the kind of clientele that might appreciate her style and talents. However, neither Alexis or Janvier even noticed her, even though she too was clad in a shiny white dress; they were too absorbed by the strange and terrifying happening this evening seemed to promise them.

So they hiked back and forth along the two sides of rue Saint-Denis passing the flow of cars between Sainte-Catherine and Ontario, Alexis with his hands thrust into his pockets and Janvier clutching his precious package under his arm.

After making a few rounds up and down this circuit that they saw as a sort of slowed down carnival, their long tramp having been carried out in mutual silence, the two men stopped at the corner of Ontario to turn northward.

"Come on! I can't dillydally any longer," Alexis said, crossing Ontario Street right then and there and heading north.

They marched a bit further up the east side of Saint-Denis as far as a seemingly anonymous and everyday rooming house.

Here, their movements became less hurried; they strode up the steps and along the halls in a determined way, but they seemed to be measuring out each step they made to give themselves time to reflect.

On the fourth floor, they paused between several doors until Janvier noticed a small black sign painted in yellow hanging beneath the round window on the last door at the end of the hallway. Here was written:

MAGUS PICHU
MASTER OF MAGIC

Rue St-Denis

This made Janvier smirk, but without his face relaxing whatsoever, for his looks grew more severe. He also held more securely his strange package wrapped in brown paper, now virtually concealing it under his forearm. Not really knowing at all what he was getting into, Alexis was watching, all around him, for signs of the occult. The both of them were terribly apprehensive. They had, of course, had similar experiences in the timber yards when they were still young in the Gaspé region, or on the Saint Lawrence seaway project ... and then, in prison!

It was quite clearly the persistent memory of an immense injustice that gave them the courage to apply three loud knocks on the Magus's door. This injustice, along with a thirst for revenge, was for undeserved years in prison as well as for the ghastly death of their youngest sister, Fabienne, named "the saint" in the family. The justice system had found them both guilty of her death.

The man who came to answer the door was both taller and more rugged than Alexis and Janvier. Ensconced in a fine black velvet suit, his hands large and fingers bony, his face scarred and with his hair sleeked down, he seemed to step right out of some American thriller ... to such a point that the two Gaspé boys were quite surprised to hear him say in impeccable French ...

"Can I help you, gentlemen?"

"We have a rendezvous with Mister Pichu," said Alexis.

"Master Pichu," the tall dark man interjected.

"Master Pichu," Janvier concurred, fumbling about with his package.

The three men were standing in a small green room flanked with tan-coloured corduroy chairs. On the walls, in aptly arranged frames, cabalistic signs were on display along with ancient maps and texts, Tarot cards and scenes from the Middle Ages giving this waiting room, on the one hand, a luxurious veneer that rendered the squalid hallway less noticeable and, on the other hand, added a note of mystery that would no doubt imbue any clients with a feeling of novelty and magic. This would surely increase the Master's charisma and encourage spectacular results.

"Please be kind enough to wait a few moments. I'll inform the Master that you are here."

The one whom the two Gaspé boys saw as a sort of bodyguard rather than a secretary vanished through a dark doorway hidden behind a thick brown baize curtain leaving the two men dressed in white alone for the last time. However, the latter did not look at each other, nor did they speak. The die was cast and they didn't want to lower the gun barrel they had just levelled at the catalyst ... of their unjust fate!

And of the *saint's*!

A few minutes later, when the warder came back to lead them into the Master's headquarters, they were sure revenge was on the way. They passed into a rather small room with walls and ceiling painted black. A thick black carpet covered the entire floor. In the centre of the room, a small low fluorescent green table stood among three little black cushions. A lamp forming a regular dodecahedron hung above the table casting a series of constantly moving beams, for the lamp, due to the wind gusting through a window opening onto Saint-Denis, made a gentle rotation. Through this window, as well, the brightly flashing sign of the neighbouring tourist rooms were to be seen.

The red glow repeatedly cast into the tiny room recalled something like the dramatic passing of an ambulance or a police car. This increased the room's strangeness. Only the noises rising from the street maintained a sense of everyday life.

The three men were waiting: the unobtrusive assistant to the Master, standing next to some black drapes that probably concealed a doorway, and the two customers, glimmering in the artificial darkness.

Suddenly, an odour of incense escaped from beneath the heavy drapery. Then, the Master emerged holding in his left hand a little silver spoon in which a cube of incense was bobbing about; he immediately balanced this in the centre of the table on a small flat plate, it also silver.

Wearing a wide white robe that amplified his own corpulence, the Master, a man of about sixty, had a hammer-shaped face, his head circled with a wavy crown of white hair, his eyes pale and terrifying, his lips thick and his mouth showing saw-like white teeth. He was a good head taller than his two visitors.

With a single discreet but effective wave, he had his two guests sit before him. Then, with another gesture, less warm and rather more authoritarian, he sent his hired hand to pull the blinds, close the window and lower the dark blind decorated with a huge oriental serpent in the same shade of green as the low table.

Alexis and Janvier felt as though they were surrounded. The last link with daylight, not to say with reality, had just faded away.

After a leaden silence infused with Oriental music apparently flowing from all six wall surfaces at once, the Magus was the first to speak, closing his eyelids as though in deep reflection:

"Do you have the little package?"

Without the slightest hesitation, Janvier held out the brown package that he had been pawing since the early afternoon. However, the Master didn't stir and didn't concern himself with the bundle. Then, it was the ever-present — although even more discreet — man in black who, having softly approached, leaned over Janvier's shoulder and, passing his horrible left hand before the Gaspé boy's face, pressed his thumb against his index and middle fingers, whispering:

"The money!"

Janvier, who felt he was being quite naïve not to have marked the difference between the small and large packages, rapidly pulled out a little well-filled envelop that again he held out to the Master. However, for the second time, the Magus didn't budge. Again, the man in black intervened to nimbly seize the despicable money. Still in meditation, the Master of Magic stretched out his hand, the left one this time, and asked for the brown package. Janvier placed it deftly in his hand, but the Master held it immediately out to Alexis while the man in black, speaking for the Master, asked Alexis to unwrap it.

Alexis, rather taxed by this process, understood nonetheless the significance of this request. When, once the package was opened, he discovered the long and round white cloth doll, his eyes hardened and he passed the doll roughly over to the Master of Magic, thus sharing with Janvier the spirit of revenge and the responsibility for their actions.

At the very moment that the eyes of the two men crossed, they again heard the voice of the man in black — a raspy low voice, a bit the affected voice of a theatre narrator ... . an almost monk-like *recto tono* voice.

"The Master agrees to apply his just powers so as to serve your cause. May the moral as well as the crucial responsibility remain yours and yours alone, for it is solely up to you to break the thread that ties the object of your hatred to life, the Master being only a catalyst for your will to destroy. Concentrate. Withdraw into yourselves and into the depths of your hatred. Without the complete consent of your spirit of revenge, the Master can do nothing, for you alone will know the victim of the Master's power and of your profound desire to cause someone to die. Concentrate then. Concentrate as you search for the epitome of your hatred. Set your mind upon it so that your conscious being is completely immersed in it."

Then, the Master of Magic broke into a sort of dirge, its syllables closely resembling the babble of a child. This primitive song, unleashed vehemently and unexpectedly, caused Alexis to stiffen and thoroughly lose his concentration. He was seized with the theatrical showiness of the scene— the dark surroundings, the low fluorescent table, the Master and his two clients all dressed in white and the scarred subordinate lurking in the shadows ... the music, the singing, the incense ... Magus Pichu's ritualistic movements ... the white plump doll made of cotton and serge embodying the purpose, the goal of this venture for which Alexis was gradually losing his enthusiasm. Just at that moment, despite the fact that Alexis hadn't stirred one iota in his bewilderment and was still maintaining his meditative posture, the Magus broke off from his chant and sharply addressed the Gaspé man stating again that, without his compliance, he was helpless, that his destructive powers would be nullified if he didn't direct all of his pain, his vengeful feelings, indeed, even his cruelest aims towards the person he wanted to destroy ... that this wished for death would only be brought about if the four of them, through their will power, succeeded in disrupting this distant target's breath of life!

Then, the chant was taken up again, accompanied by a long modulated dirge coming from the man in black. Soon, the two Gaspé boys sensed some form of hovering flight that next expanded into an image of gloomy vultures above a prey unconscious of the destructive powers now weighing down upon it! A prey unaware that a violent gust was slowly pushing it towards the edge of an abyss ... And this induced them to believe that their revenge was only a step away.

However, though this was happening, it didn't really last, for time, like matter, was giving more and more scope to an intense and violent inner experience fixed upon the destruction of a past evil still reverberating in the present.

It was the Master of Magic alone, with his eyes half-closed, who drove a violently icy gaze into the white doll, a replica of the victim, at the same time he held it tensely in the palm of his left hand, his fingers ready to crush its throat.

The more the minutes passed, the more the two brothers steeped themselves in their pain, thus intensifying their need for vengeance. As well, as for Master Pichu and his trusty deacon in magic — like lugubrious birds shrouding misfortune under their diabolical wings — the more they tore into the silence with their coordinated chanting, the more they decimated the time separating this ceremony and the still remote scene that would bring revenge for the two men in white.

Later, when midnight sounded in the rest of the time zone, each of them had lost any notion of time. Their movements and thoughts were purely reflective, clearly centred on some kind of clay pigeon to be shot down as soon as it was identified! Exactly this did happen quite dramatically at an hour when only a few night birds were still wandering about rue Saint-Denis.

It was Janvier who was the first to start. With a violent rush, accompanied by a primitive and prolonged shriek rising from the back of his throat, he struck his two fists sharply against the low table. Immediately, the Magus reared up while Alexis repeated Janvier's cry and carried out the same gestures two or three times over.

The man in black added his voice to the common howl while his knees gave way in a nervous spasm. At that very moment, the Master of Magic, grasping the white doll more firmly, drew from his right sleeve a long shiny hat pin, a needle that sparkled with a light soon cloaked by the white cotton fetish doll.

Next, the Magus, still in a trance, furiously brandished the needle and, before plunging it into the symbolic pile of cotton, he vigorously squeezed the doll's throat.

Then and there, a cry rose from his own throat and his eyes rolled heavenward.

He hadn't the time to realize that he was, simultaneously, on the right end and the wrong end of his monstrous weapon that lay in his power just as the needle pierced the doll that was his own effigy! His whole being then crumpled and his body slumped forward. The kamikaze doll tucked between his arms and his abdomen and pierced by the death-dealing needle was no longer visible.

The next moment, suddenly aroused, exhausted and sweating profusely, the two boys from the Gaspé opened their eyes. It didn't take long for them to realize that their scheme had worked.

However, just as Janvier was about to lean over the collapsed body of the person they had taken so many months to trace down, a heavy muscular form crushed him against the green table. It was the man in black who was endeavouring to pull the needle out of the doll. Alexis then came to his brother's rescue, yanking at the legs of Master of Magic's helper and a brawl ensued.

The man in black, thoroughly enraged, was very difficult to hold at bay; the two brothers, though experienced in this kind of combat, were promptly knocked about by the man with the scar, with Alexis even causing the Magus's body to be sent flying.

Next, spotting the flashing needle that was thrust clean through the white doll, he tore it from the clump of cotton and rushed upon their adversary with a last gasp of energy. Then, the latter crashed to the ground with the fatal weapon glistening between his shoulder blades. Following this, the long dark body gave a few twitches and twisted about a moment before writhing into a ball; it lay perfectly still in the silence with the needle pointing directly towards the Master of Magic.

The two brothers, totally played out, crumbled to the floor. This time, the occult had played no part in their killing! The weapon, left in the wound, still shone in the middle of this dark room.

Suddenly, a faint moan from the Magus brought them back to their feet. It was Janvier who reflected on what would wipe out any trace of the fact they were killers! In fact, taking hold of the Master of Magic's body, they brought it to lie along side the man in black and, while the Master, in a last breath, was murmuring,: "Now, I recognize you," they tightened his hand once again on the needle, thereby extinguishing his deadly splendour ...

Then, they went out to walk until dawn, looking for some relief ... and some new meaning for their lives.

Perhaps they were going to make a real saint out of the *saint?*

Rue St-Denis

The Heaven-sent World Map

*Everything has a beginning,
a middle and an end.*
Aristotle

Georges du Tarn was born in the Aveyron in 1896 and had been living in Quebec since 1968 after having spent thirty years in China. (He had come to be with his daughter, Isabelle, married to a Quebecker from the Eastern Townships). He was now living in lowly conditions, having retired to a patch of land in Dorchester county where he managed to grow his eggplants and make wine from dandelions, carrots, beets and raspberries.

For several days, Georges du Tarn had to look after his grandson, Eugene. That morning, he took little Eugene out with him somewhere along the end of the property of his grumbly neighbour, "father LaToux." Both were off hunting for frogs while filling their bags as well with dandelions. Of course, if they were to come upon a hare or a partridge, Georges was a very good shot.

Precisely at this moment, in Montreal, Isabelle Brochu, born du Tarn, for she was Georges' daughter, was running across rue Saint-Denis just where it crosses Maisonneuve Boulevard; meanwhile, in Verchères, Marcel Brochu, her husband, was tenderly watching two six or seven year old children as they dipped their boots in the river.

Once again at this very moment, in Millau, Georges' birthplace, another du Tarn, Edmonde Pucci, Georges' sister, swaying her body heavily from one leg to the other, was painfully making her way across the Lerouge Bridge, watching the water rushing beneath her feet.

In Paris, Marceline Boutu, another of Georges' daughters, was waiting for Edmond Boutu at the Odeon. Edmond was twenty minutes late.

In Nancy, Martin du Tarn, Georges' grandson and the son of Raoul, was running across Stanislas Square with two security men on his tail.

In Strasbourg, Léontine Loehner, another of du Tarn's daughters, was stepping out of the tobacco shop in Rome Street with some Gauloises for her Gustav, an employee for Strasbourg Gas.

And in Peking, Ye Kou-Wang, Georges du Tarn's illegitimate daughter, was writing a ta-tse-bao in honour of her factory council in a tiny street inaccessible to tourists.

It's a thing difficult to explain without being somehow shaken but let us just say that, starting from this moment, Georges du Tarn and his grandson were once again quite completely alone in the world! That is to say they were the only ones to be still conscious and simultaneously involved in both space and time, for all the rest of the universe had suddenly ceased to move.

What is more, Georges was quite clearly aware of this fact as he manoeuvred his way through father LaToux' cow fence. He was first of all astonished by the absence of any wind. Then, by the sight of the trees and hay bent over as though the wind was still blowing. And then, there was the heavy and oppressive silence. Even Eugene sensed instinctively a certain malaise. Neither of them had time to share their impressions. Before them, indeed, as black as teak, as square as a die and as smooth as marble, a strange mass hovered in space at approximately a man's height.

The object neither moved nor emitted the anything at all. Both the man and the child were awestruck. They remained motionless for some seconds, even though Georges had, for a mere instant, the idea of running off to the village to alert the mayor and the chief of police. But what if, meanwhile, this mass were to fly off! What would he look like? Like one of those oddballs who start shouting about flying saucers on the slightest provocation. Then, as well, he wasn't too sure his old legs would carry him all the way there and then back. And so he decided to stay.

Then, slowly, as though he were still on the hunt, he began quite cautiously to approach the object, stepping lightly and holding the boy protectively against him; the boy, Eugene, who, believing he was in the middle of some summer night's dream, quite reasonably tempered his own fears. However, a few steps away from "the thing," Georges preferred to go on alone, and he left Eugene behind him.

From this moment onward, walking became strangely more difficult; not having to protect the child quite so closely as well, he felt less confident, more vulnerable. But there was scarcely time now to think of such things.

At an arm's distance from the black mass, he began to make out its texture; he thought of a sort of dust or spatial earth in a state of advanced decomposition. Soot in a sort of solid form!

He carefully picked up an end of dry branch, taking care not to move too hastily; then, nervously, though with great precaution, he held out the branch before him. As he touched the object, he foolishly dropped it! Was he afraid of being contaminated or electrocuted, or of being struck by some atomic force? Perhaps it was simply a fear of the unknown? He really didn't know himself.

Now, at that very moment, several things occurred.

First of all, the mass spread out over the ground, burning the grassy surface and itself turning into dust, a very unusual dust!

At this same instant as well, the rest of the world began to move again, imperceptively and at a very slow speed, so that, from now to the end of this tale, humanity will have only managed to stir the end of its toes ...

Unless it be that Georges and Eugene's movements were being carried out in some more hurried situation.

Again Georges du Tarn was tempted to dash off to the village, although he rejected doing so for the same reasons he had before. A few minutes went by during which neither Georges nor his grandson made the slightest move ... well, scarcely any at all. Quite dumbfounded, they were gazing upon this heaven-sent world globe without questioning really too much where it had come from. It crashed to the ground a few steps behind the child who cried out:

"It's exactly like some geographic map!"

Indeed, the black mass which had now disintegrated, took the shape of a world map! Yes, a map of the world. One, after all, of this earth, and not in any outline form, but in all its details!

Next, the old man approached it and agreed that it was indeed a geographic map. Picking up his stick again, he went about explaining to the boy some details about the world and his own life.

He first of all looked over the dusty map without touching it and, as the child asked him where Montreal was, that far away town his mother so often left him for long days at a time, the grandfather placed the end of his improvised pointer on a spot in the river, this spot suddenly disappeared from the map! Just as though the tiny clump of dust in that space had penetrated scorched soil!

At that exact instant, on rue Saint-Denis, a long fissure appeared close to the left foot of Isabelle Brochu, her maiden name being du Tarn. A fissure which, in no time at all, swallowed up streets, houses and citizens. Montreal suddenly disappeared, sinking away into the river as though some uncontrollable mass had come to wipe out the entire island, as though its very foundations had been shattered! At Verchères as well, two children in their booties, Marcel Brochu and numerous others, were swept down into the abyss ... to the west as far as Saint-Zotique!

After allowing some of his memories to float around on the surface of his consciousness and unaware of the devilish catastrophe that he was unfurling upon the world, Georges du Tarn pointed with the end of his stick at south-central France but without pressing it since he wasn't absolutely sure he had the right spot. Then, as quick as a wink, he coldly pressed the end down where he believed he recognized Millau moving it as far as this other location which he thought to be Paris.

"When I was nineteen years of age, I went to live in Paris with your grandmother."

In reality, he touched on the very centre of Millau, skimmed Saint-Flour and Clermont-Ferrand to the west, Montluçon and Bourges to the east and just grazed Paris.

That very instant, at Millau, Edmonde Pucci, Renaldo Pucci's widow and a sister to Georges, could feel a strange reeling sensation at the back of her eyes and down in her stomach. She lost consciousness before the Lerouge Bridge slipped away beneath her feet.

In Paris, Marceline Boutu, formerly a du Tarn, became suddenly aware of the close proximity of the world's end, just as

Edmond Brochu was sticking the end of his rather longish nose out the Saint-Germain exit of the Odeon metro stop. As for Edmond, he had no time to be aware, struggling as he was to fight his way out of the mob.

Then, as Georges du Tarn's pointer stirred about with a stroke that snuffed out the dusty material as it went, (we hasten to repeat this for it's important) this stroke turned sharply towards Nancy and Strasbourg ...

"When your grandmother died, at the birth of your uncle Ralph, in thirty seven, I sent the children to relatives in Nancy and Strasbourg ... "

And just at that very moment, as he was making a few strides along Stanislas Square, Martin du Tarn, Georges' grandson had a vague but persistent sensation of tightness in his chest. Right away he thought he should come to a halt but he didn't have time to. Likewise, in Strasbourg, Léontine Loehner, another du Tarn, saw a strange glow of light above the university buildings ...

"Then, I left here for Peking ... "

Old Georges raised his slim branch and leaned over to place it directly on the spot he thought to be Peking.

Just then, Ye Kou-Wang, the illegitimate child of a foreigner, scarcely had the time herself to guess that her country and people were being somehow attacked. Every light around her had gone dim. Everything inside her darkened as well.

At the end of this brief but convincing exposé, the boy, Eugene, saw his grandfather in a different light. He could sense the adventurous beast at work in this stern looking man with a tanned complexion and sparse white hair. And probably so as to preserve this impression of greatness, and maybe as well, merely to maintain verbal contact, little Eugene added rather unconsciously:

"Then, after that?"

"After that ... Well now, after several years spent in loving people, I came here to be with your mother who had just given birth to you. Here ... "

Along with this, he buried the end of his stick on the "kamikaze" world map at Sainte-Sabine in Dorchester county ... With Georges du Tarn being completely unaware of the planet-wide reverberations of his actions, the strange world map rushed away to become blurred in its own abyss. And there was no longer any one in existence who would be able to give any evidence of this world.

Although, to tell the truth, this world map ...

André Carpentier

Bi's Bell

(...) the large financial institutions have made loans well beyond their capacity. Credit has its limits. Speculators begin to doubt. Everyone wants to sell his shares before they lose their value.There's panic in the New York Stock Exchange, then in every stock exchange throughout the world. Companies slow down their production, through lack of capital as well as markets, buyers having also lost their credit. Factories grind to a halt, unemployment is rampant. No longer is there work, production or consumption. Capitalism has known recessions before this one but never as serious as this. They call it the 1929 Depression and it will last through the thirties.
Léandre Bergeron *The Little Quebec History Manual*

Nineteen thirty-two. Montreal, like the rest of the world, was in the midst of an economic crisis which became all the more deadly every day that passed.

While the open air *golden tramway* made its way through Montreal's rumbling arteries, showing the town to the few tourists still present as well as to the local shopkeeper class, while the streetcars, bicycles, autos and the last horse-drawn carriages were competing for space in the streets, on the sidewalks and a bit everywhere, in front of groceries, butchers and bakeries, men, women and children, harbouring welfare coupons, formed line-ups of endless distress and misfortune. Poverty was collecting in droves. People traded coupons and sold their souls for a mouthful of bread.

From taverns to coffee shops, Montreal's mayor, Camilien Houde, was establishing his jocular popularity; the underworld and local financiers were profiting from American prohibition.

In Quebec, the Taschereau government, in the hopes of ridding their cities of unemployed, launched an umteenth campaign for a return to the land and for a settlement on uncultivated and sometimes untillable patches of ground. Maurice Duplessis was making his first inroads in politics.

In Ottawa, MacKenzie King, a former advisor in industrial relations to Rockefeller, found himself momentarily in the Opposition while Bennet and his Conservatives had just voted, two years previously, for a twenty million dollar budget to have the unemployed look after public works.

Meanwhile, Woodworth founded the CCF and Aberhart Social Credit; Lionel Groulx advocated the "revenge of the cradles" crossbred with an enlightened dictatorship in a French-speaking state linked to the Commonwealth, a state to be called, *Laurentia*!

The working class didn't understand anything of all this except that they were the turkeys in this farce weathering the crisis under great gusts of collective misery and shame.

Industry was almost completely paralysed, unemployment grew more widespread; even American investors fired their workers out on to the streets after settling on their property. One hundred thousand were on relief.

People responded to the crisis each in his own way: with work or despair or some kind of adventure.

Now, during this cool period in the month of October, a young man only a few steps away from complete despair, like so many others, had come to choose adventure; however, not just any at all, but the most perilous kind, one that borders on magic, ghosts and the diabolical. The curé of his village, downcast at seeing a naive scarcely twenty-two year old country boy plunge alone into the great venture of city living during such a difficult period, economically speaking, had himself arranged a small trip for the young man to his own mother's home so as to bring him to the port of Quebec, "on the doorstep of despair," as he put it.

This young man, whose first name was really Arsène, but who was better known by the nickname, Bi, for he was the youngest in a family of sixteen from the county of Lotbinière, this young man then, fairly smart and quite enterprising, according to his fellows, was mad after adventure and ready for anything, so long as it was honest, to get himself and his family out of this poverty over which he wasn't himself overly indignant — for it was the fate of everyone around him — but it made life appear quite sad and pointless.

Indeed, it wasn't just by chance or as a result of some mere whim that Bi had freed himself from his mother's apron strings and from the fetters of a kind though authoritarian father. On the contrary, he had been waiting for the occasion for more than a year, but the right one, one that would be most advantageous, not just some wretched trip on the back of a train meandering towards the Canadian west or northern USA!

And there it was, he had it! What is more, it had been given him by the curé of his own village.

So, one October afternoon, while watching the old boys in the village play spades at the corner store and listening to them

Rue St-Denis

relate their age-old fantastic tales so typical of the region, the good curé, who had stopped off to greet his old companions, didn't like being outdone following a particularly vibrant and dramatic tale by old man Doris. And so, he had himself declared that there had been in Montreal, or to be more exact, on rue Saint-Denis, the authentic case of a haunted house, said to be the house "with the bell."

How about that: nothing less than a haunted house! And that wasn't all. This house, where no one had lived for nearly ten years, was to be given away! Not to be sold, the old curé affirmed, but to be awarded for nothing! Provided, of course, that you underwent the terrible test of living in it for a few hours. And up till then, the curé added, no one had walked out of it alive.

Indeed, nothing more was required for the passionate and dauntless spirit of Bi to become quite stirred, then to set up a campaign plan and announce to everybody his departure for the big city!

Upon his arrival at the port of Montreal, on one of the rare merchant ships still coming from Quebec, Bi had gone straight to the Meurling shelter on Saint-Paul Street near the market. There he dined and spent his first night.

The next day, proud and quite sure of himself, allowing his dark mane which was too long for the times to float in the dusty city air like some diabolical halo around his tweed cap, he took off in the direction of rue Saint-Denis in search of the famous haunted house. But then, sun and wind joined harmonious forces to create a radiant morning that made him feel like dreaming and loafing about ... Dreaming of an easy life, sheltered from cold and hunger, for himself, his sisters and his brothers, dreaming of a life on four cushy tires, with a pretty wife on his arm wearing an orchid on her blouse.

That day too, Bi, preferring his dream to reality, had been content to walk down Saint-Jacques Street, passing close by the pillars of the larger banks. Then, in the evening he had gone to line-up at the "Soup Works", before the convent of the Sisters of Providence on Saint-Hubert Street. Now, the line up that evening was so particularly long that it snaked its way all the way back to Sainte-Catherine Street, so that, when it came to his turn, there were no longer any beds.

And so, still faithful to his image as a wily headstrong country boy, he had proposed his services directly to sister Bonneau who had no doubt accepted this offer on the spot. Thus it was that, after a bowl of soup, a car came to get him, along with a few others, to take them to the corner of Aylwin and Ontario, in the centre of the Hochelaga district where these sisters looked after the aged and chronically ill.

Bi worked here for three days for room and board, using a piece of flannel to wash the old folks down, playing a violin and harmonica for them in the evenings and, on the quiet, transporting the dead to the morgue on Saint-Vincent Street.

Then, one morning, at dawn on the fourth day, feeling his faith melting as fast as his girth, he decided to leave this scene, both physically and morally one of heartache, ailment and distress, to run off and stake everything on witchcraft and risk his very life in a mad and futile hope to defeat misery.

He marched across the city from east to west until reaching the slopes of Saint-Denis on the eastern side.

After a few moments, when he could feel his encounter with the fantastic approaching, he began to mutter and gasp; he inhaled the smoke of his first cigarette, which made him a bit dizzy, then, throwing back his shoulders, his gave his forward stride an air both determined and unassailable.

Rue St-Denis

And so, he finally arrived before the notorious haunted house.

It was a rather ordinary place with a stone facade and several wooden steps which gave it the appearance of a boarding house. Only a small hand-painted wooden sign informed passers-by as to the magical, be it diabolical character of this apparently uninteresting residence.

Indeed, Bi was rather disappointed since he had been expecting archways, porches and skylights, dark gardens dotted with silent pools and perhaps even a family vault. The cool weather didn't at all fit in with his thoughts of thunder, lightning and drenching rain.

Then, an old man with an engaging smile came up to him, followed by his wife with a tender gaze. Bi didn't hesitate to explain the reasons for his visit nor were they long in pointing out to him how things really worked thereabouts.

The old woman kept repeating to him how young he was to be rushing into such an adventure, while the man with a toothless grin went on saying:

"Maybe so, but at least, whatever happens, for him, poverty is over!"

How things worked? Well, then! If Bi were to succeed in getting as far as a little pink bedroom on the second floor and would then ring a bell he would find there, the house was his! Would this break the magic spell? At worst, he told himself, I could exploit the place as all these good folks have been doing!

"That will be a hundred dollars," said the old fellow holding out his hand ...

"A hundred dollars!" Bi said with stupefaction.

The old village priest hadn't spoken to him about that! And, of course, he had not at all even one of these hundred dollars in his pocket. So, both insulted and frustrated, he began sounding off quite shamelessly about theft and deceit. His mouth frothed with rancour and his howls and gestures of rage lured a crowd that, drawn by the smell of blood, often hurried to be present at the onset of someone caught in this devilish trap.

Right away people started yelling "Let him in," "Give him a chance" ... But the old couple refused to let their feelings get the better of them. A man stepped from the crowd to the applause and cries of all and sundry: "Here's the old sawbones," the mob cried. "Let him in, doctor ... give him his chance ... just as you had yours before ... "

Then, stammering, the man who was one-armed and wearing a dapper navy-blue suit, made an open-handed gesture in the hopes of calming the quarrelsome whims of the indolent crowd, and this in turn called forth their cries of joy: "three cheers for the good doctor," "Hurrah for the daring young country lad ... " meanwhile, the old woman, standing on the step and cupping her hands to carry her voice, shouted:

"The young man will try his luck! Come and see youth up against the powers of magic! Hurry now, my good people ... "

And while Bi was mounting the steps one by one, spying fearfully into the inner hallway, the crowd hovered outside as judges and witnesses to his adventure. And the old lady began selling crepes and beans, and the old man local beer and wood alcohol, for folks often came a good way to stand in front of the haunted house to await the fate of some audacious countryman!

As soon as Bi was inside, the door closed with a sinister thump. For a moment, his eyes had to adjust to the half-light. He next found the decor rather inoffensive. This house certainly didn't give the impression it was haunted or bewitched!

In any case, he knew he shouldn't forget his objective which was to ring the bell on the second floor. He immediately rushed up the stairs. However, this was to his regret for, as fast as he could speak, he found himself on the floor his brain pounding with a violent headache! Though he hadn't noticed, the top of the stairs had been blocked in! As well, he had struck the top of his skull against a panel of wooden beams. This should quite clearly serve him a good lesson! Evidently, there was something more cunning than himself at work in this house.

So he set off in search of a stairway, for it was only logical that there must be one leading upwards.

Now, there were only two large rooms on that floor and neither of them seemed to conceal a staircase. He tapped on the walls, piled up furniture to examine the ceilings, even opened a cupboard ... and just as, unawares, he was about to close one of the doors, he felt himself grasped, as though his arm were being seized by some flimsy but unyielding substance; it was a kind of long dark cassock whose sleeves were attempting to hold him by encircling his wrist!

His first reflex was to slam the door shut against these blood-soaked arms and to throw all his weight as well as that of the door to hold those life-like shreds at bay! After a few seconds, quite exhausted and highly unnerved, Bi found himself on the floor, free but still stunned! He had just understood what the word "haunted" really meant ...

Next, still on all fours and painfully struggling for breath, his gaze fell upon a slim iron foot from which there came a strange grating sound; he raised his eyes slowly towards a piece of mediaeval armour until the entire thing loomed into view holding a sort of halberd aimed at the ceiling. Then, he just had time to roll away when the weapon was already planted in the floor, flush in the shadow of his shoulder!

He needed to think, so he backed against a bare wall in order to be sure he would see any new attempt on him coming his way.

But just as his back pressed against the slick wall, he felt he was losing his balance! And indeed, the wall swung about on itself like a revolving door and Bi fell back on a hard and uneven surface; he had jarred a rib and a hip bone but, what was more important, he had also discovered the staircase, secluded and camouflaged away in a dark dusty recess! This would surely spare him numerous efforts and save him from some other attack.

Then, with infinite caution, he began to clamber up the stairs. No doubt about it, this house was not only haunted but rigged as well on all sides with booby traps.

His restraint now served him well for, several times over, the irregular height of the steps forced him to swerve about rather dangerously. The stairs, made of iron and cement, were quite steep. At another moment, when nearly at the top, he slightly missed his footing and tried to grab onto a thin panel close at hand but only succeeded in gashing his fingers.

On the landing a new hallway flanked with doorways, suggesting everything that could possibly seem weird and mysterious, lay before him.

Without really watching too attentively and thereby leaving everything up to chance, he chose the farthest door. He then stepped forward and gently turned the handle and pushed the heavy structure wide open.

In a split second, Bi was completely dazzled by the intensity of the light pouring out from beyond this doorway, but he nonetheless made the unconscious venture of taking a step forward. It was at that very moment that, before he really understood what was happening, he sensed a complete void beneath his feet! Instinctively, — and it was this that saved him — he grabbed the door frame with both hands! His head then swung slightly inside. He was then terrified by what he heard and saw: about twenty feet below, the crowd met earlier, now eating and guzzling away, had their gaze fixed upon him! When they observed him hanging onto the door's edge, the people, still surrounding the smiling old couple, uttered a long sorrowful disenchanted moan. He slammed the door violently shut with his eyes riveted upon the bloodstain he had just left on the panelling ...

He then crept back along the narrow hallway which he had crossed too rapidly for him to have really seen it, a hallway crowned with an immense chandelier. However, he was brought quickly to a halt by the sight of two shiny black ... almost metallic ... cats!

The three of them, standing stock still, stared at one another for a good moment, the animals giving no sign of life whatever and Bi sweating profusely in the damp cold of this virtually deserted house. Then, judging that he could wait no longer, he made up his mind to slink around these two cats. However — and this was to be expected — when Bi was but two steps away, they began showing some signs of life ... violent ones! They both revealed two white and sharply pointed rows of teeth and leapt on Bi with all their fangs and claws in view. But Bi, who had foreseen this manoeuvre, received the two creatures with a violent thrust of his forearm which sent this crashing against one of the side doors and, under the impact, these flew open ... At that very instant, with no forewarning and as if by magic, two sharp iron rods sprang from the door frame and another from the doorstep itself! Bi found himself caught between two shafts of iron, one having torn into a piece of his shoulder and the other, striking a bit of his cheek and an eye! Besides, one of the vertical rods had quite nicely impaled one of the two cats which proved then and there to be purely mechanical — a mechanism now wedged in the upper part of the door! But Bi didn't see this, distressed as he was with the pain and the lunacy of his actions ...

Next, before he could manage to escape from this iron mesh trap, he began to feel a series of nibbles in his left leg.. It was the second cat clawing him and quite callously biting away at his ankle! As well, as though to intensify his suffering, a shower of finely sharpened darts immediately rained down from the chandelier and shredded his leg and simultaneously wiped out the second mechanical cat.

Then, things happened quite swiftly.

First, with a howl of despair that made the spectators outside shiver, Bi slipped frantically down into the room observed through his bloody eye. Now borne along by his reptilian movements, he collided with a full-length mirror which, thanks to its blue-tinted glass and art nouveau frame, he hadn't noticed! What he did see, however, was his right arm crashing through the glass, so that it was lost forever! His arm had been shorn of its substance! He had only a shred of flesh hanging from his shoulder ... a lifeless scarlet shred!

His blood was everywhere and the pain was so penetrating it seemed to flow from no particular source. Within a few seconds, he appeared to have lost an eye, an arm and a leg!

His head reeling, Bi then attempted to make his way to the exit, but, as he went, he could feel something prickly and sinuous against his face just above his wounds. This sudden pain also made him writhe about so that he bumped against a sort of empty drum; an intense boom then reverberated beyond the house. While, in the middle of the pinkish room, he examined the object that had skimmed his face, that is to say, a three-ply cable linked to a bronze clock, the drum went on uninterruptedly with the same booming report following quite closely the rhythm of Bi's own heartbeat.

During the minutes that followed, the even more dense

crowd huddled before the house "with the bell" could hear the sharp sound of the drum slowly speeding up its rhythm until, in a short time, it turned into a sharper rumble.

Then, precisely at noon, the bell gave a loud peal, a single clang that made everyone jump, above all the old man and his lady ... At that very same instant, the rumbling of the drum went dead!

It was only several hours later, long after the crowd had dispersed, seemingly satisfied though quite frustrated, that the old master of the haunted house found Bi's cold mutilated body ... hanging from the bell's cable! Bi who had refused to give up a part of himself for a certain shred of hope ...

Until the day it was demolished several years later, this house which was henceforth known as "Bi's home" for he had indeed deserved this memento, remained completely boarded up and no one was to enter it again ... neither the old man nor the old woman, nor the one-armed sawbones, nor the children in the district along with bums, ghosts busters or demon hunters.

Even today, when October comes along, as for certain people who are more open towards fantastic events than others and who come and stroll down rue Saint-Denis, they are sometimes able to hear a single sharp ring of a bell at noon time, Bi's bell.

ANDRÉ CARPENTIER

MADAM CORRIVEAU'S CHEST

To Francis T.

I wish for a culture that plays hooky, has its nose covered with jam, wears its hair bushy, has baggy pants and seeks in the underbrush of the imaginary the path of desire.

Henri Laborit
"In Praise Of Flight"

It was the first day of summer. A marvellous sunshine hovered over Montreal announcing a mood that was carefree, leisurely and frivolous. Some people were wearing small light shoes, others tee shirts or fringed Bermuda shorts; still others, flowery hats or plastic sunglasses.

For a few days now, secretaries dressed in summer colours could be seen, at the foot of the tall buildings down town, getting their faces tanned with the sun's rays using slim aluminium reflectors that they held below their chins.

On the west side of town, Crescent Street was swarming with alluring haughty young girls elegantly decked out; some were consciously unkempt and still others, innocently prim. However,

Rue St-Denis

all were subject to the dictatorial and expensive styles found in the surrounding shops. All around, of course, there were slim dudes, famished young wolves game for anything and music hall intellectuals as well ...

To the east, on rue Saint-Denis, the numerous terraces were teaming with another highly agitated crowd; in other words, much the same thing as on Crescent Street but in the style of the east.

Mado Brisson and Benoît Simard were living in the downstairs of a Maple Street duplex, a bit more in the north-east of the city, a duplex that Benoît would have liked to buy if it hadn't been for what he called Mado's extravagant and basically bohemian character. Since both were teachers, he at Old Montreal College, she at Rosemont, he considered they had the means to be property owners. However, Mado didn't see things that way. As she was fond of saying, she preferred to live for now, for the immediate rather than a hypothetical future or for an even more hypothetical retirement. It must be said as well that, quite clearly, Mado and Benoît were at a crossroads. Besides this, over the last several months, they had often wondered if they should continue living together. Each of them believed that they should, provided that the other one changed his or her style of living!

Benoît reproached her for not taking care of the house and for running through their income. "This isn't the way we're going to get ahead," he would say, and she kept wondering what he was really up to.

Mado reproached him for being too serious and lacking any imagination: "you've lost your ability to marvel," she would say. And he kept wondering what he could possibly marvel at in this lousy world!

Yes, indeed, they were at a crossroads. But, since they had gotten used to one another and believed they were in love, they experienced a deep need to converse or, when there was nothing to say, simply to be together.

So, since they were both off work for that magnificent afternoon, they decided to go into town just to stroll and chat. Like a goodly number in this rising middle class, who were hard-working and liberal in the broadest sense of the term, they craved a mixture of sunshine and asphalt, warm winds and Martinis. The terraces on rue Saint-Denis were just what was needed.

As they often liked to do, they had parked their Honda facing Saint-Louis Square, that strangely appealing park, marked both by history of the French-speaking middle class of the last century and by the long-haired members of the junior college generation, young people who were both fearful and rebellious, serious and excitable, transparent and mysterious — a youth that bore their very own image for, in them, they recognized their own shunned aspirations and disappointments. They had therefore walked down the western slope of Saint-Denis, heading towards the café terraces.

There, between Ontario Street and Maisonneuve Boulevard, bustling along excitedly, they rushed in a headlong quest for new purchases. Sitting in the sun and by the sidewalk, they had first of all eaten some small creamed kidneys at Jojo's which vaguely recalled their first tête-à-tête and dinner. Then, they went off to buy two records at the Alternatif, a *Rêve du Diable* and a Gary Burton, then, a few cut price comic books at the Encyclopaedic Bookstore; finally, two tickets for the Louise Forestier concert which was to take place in a few weeks at the Saint-Denis Theatre. All this was done as though the consumption of cultural niceties could serve both as an escape and as moral health insurance.

Finally, as it was their habit, they went to sit at a table at La

Rue St-Denis

Galoche which once again allowed them to have their feet by the sidewalk and the sun in their eyes. However, they didn't speak at all, which seemed to mean that they had already said everything there was to say ... or just about. Each of them was worried that, for the other, this silence might mean some sort of reproach, a sign of defeat or, on the other hand, a sort of moral comfort. Better still, each was wondering what this increasingly oppressive silence meant for him or herself.

And so, time went by, with these deep meditations about their silence, while the noise from the street and the bar became particularly acute at their table. It was only as five o'clock approached, when the office employees usually crowded into the terraces, that they decided to walk slowly back up Saint-Denis, on the east side this time, as they had so often done before.

After only a few steps, and perhaps only with the unconscious intention of drowning out the noise from the street, Mado began to speak. She knew right away that she had made a gaff, but it was too late. Benoît had stopped abruptly and his face was all red ... it was the same scarlet that had accompanied his most terrible bouts of anger!

"What!" he said, grinding his teeth, "go to Greece this summer when we don't even have the wherewithall to visit my sister in Saint-Boniface!"

As she raised her eyes heavenward, he launched himself into a violent diatribe which attracted a band of inquisitive gawkers on the look out for for something unusual and spectacular. In scarcely thirty seconds, he proved to her for all to see that such a trip would lead to their ruin. Next, he moved from logic to feelings, then, to threats. Acting these out would certainly lead to separation!

Thereupon, as though to regain the initiative in this debate, unless it was just done in a deliberate and premeditated fashion, she turned sharply on her heels and marched hurriedly between two store windows that stood close by.

It was a most sober shop-front, as it is often the case with businesses that count on a steady clientele. Set back from the sidewalk and virtually camouflaged by exterior stairways, it was the lair of a small unpretentious antique dealer identified only by an iron-framed wooden sign and a trade mark painted in a half circle on the store's one window. In both locations could be read: **The Treasure Seeker**.

Seeing Mado head for a shop window, Benoît could feel the astounding weight of destiny; he held his breath. What was she up to now?

For her part, Mado, showing a bold front before the crowd of onlookers, felt that she might successfully negotiate an appealing little acquisition in return for a summer at the Lake of Two Mountains rather than a trip to Greece. Some small purchase, off the cuff and done for no other reason than just to buy, like that box, for example, sitting in the window, the one called Madam Corriveau's Chest. And at a price that would soon have Greece forgotten — merely a hundred dollars.

Benoît protested vigorously. This was really going too far! And since he didn't realize that Mado considered this purchase as a consolation prize, a kind of reward for indulgence, he thought that the time had come for an ultimatum:

"No, Mado. No, no, no!"

However, she walked into the shop just the same.

"I forbid you. If you buy that box ... "

He had to break off his sentence. Mado was inside and Benoît was alone on the sidewalk.

The man who greeted Mado was rather small and thin. He was nearly bald as well and had a hooked nose. He looked rather swank with his neat moustache tinged with a few white hairs; he must have been between forty and forty-five years of age.

The man was also dressed in a most fashionable style. At first sight, he might have been taken for a tailor or a barber. Terribly affected, both in his gestures and in his speech, he gave off a sort of inner vibration suggesting magic and the occult. There was something bewitching about him. In this, his eyes, framed behind tiny round glasses, were of singular importance.

However, the little man didn't get very far conversing with Mado, for Benoît, who had been watching for a few seconds through the window, came rushing in to make a final attempt at reasoning with her.

"Mado, if you buy this box, we won't be able to pay the rent!"

"The rent, Benoît," she fired back, "can always be payed next month, whereas this box will be in someone else's living room in a month if I don't buy it ... "

These few chance remarks were enough for the man behind the counter to understand the significance of Mado's stubborn desire to buy this box. It also came to him that he should get a move on both in judging the physical qualities of the young woman and, as well, in completing this sale before Benoît could manage to talk her out of it.

He then examined her rapidly from head to toe, judging with a single glance that she was clearly much more beautiful and seductive than most of his female customers.

Deciding to play all his cards, he raised his cold slender hand from behind the counter and grasped Mado's as you might seize a beautiful volume jammed between several others ...

Mado wasn't at all astonished by this bold move. In any case, so she told herself, there probably wasn't a corner dark enough on rue Saint-Denis where she would be afraid of this phony dwarf. And then, as well, she was perhaps unconsciously ready to do anything just to annoy Benoît. The little man, still quite ingratiating, began reading the lines in the hand of this woman whom he already considered to be his newest catch!

He spoke to her of her aesthetic sense linked to a deep awareness of her roots and her patrimony ...

"You must enjoy historic articles, Miss ... "

Benoît found the scene so utterly ridiculous that, for a moment he imagined that Mado wasn't capable of falling into such a crude trap! Mado herself was rather embarrassed by this lack of openness and finesse, but she neither could nor would back off. What is more, she now encouraged the Treasure Seeker with sighs and stares.

The little man saw then, in the lines of her left hand alone, a marked fascination for mystery and a need to impress those around her..

Benoît couldn't take it any more.

"I suppose you have precisely this beautiful historic object for sale since it is so full of mystery and likely to impress our friends."

However, the seeker pretended not to hear, staring deeply into Mado's eyes and pressing the palm of her hand. Mado smiled. Benoît was quite tense and his hands were moist.

The little man took advantage of this oppressive moment of silence to come out from behind his counter and walk slowly towards the window. Mado and Benoît were then able to notice that the Treasure Seeker had a limp and a cane was tied to his left wrist, like handcuffs on a criminal ...

The room was very warm ...

On the way back to the counter, the man headed straight towards Mado and placed "Corriveau's Chest" in her hands.

Rue St-Denis

The chest was a large and curved like a lunch box. It was made of segments of varnished pine held together by a black iron framework. A small keyhole adorned its surface, but it held no key.

The man next drew a small chain from his jacket pocket and placed it around Mado's neck. The key, which was tied to it, hung just above Mado's breasts, partially concealing the copper neck band that Benoît had given her.

The latter, moreover, feeling the tension rise, jumped impetuously between Mado and the Treasure Seeker, bellowing at one of them to put an end to this inane ritual and to the other to come home with him immediately.

"Mado, it's either me or this stupid chest."

"I want this chest," she shouted, even louder, "and you're the one who's stupid!"

Like a frustrated child, Benoît brusquely stamped his foot and headed for the door, shouting: "I'm leaving!"

Mado was now alone with the little man, but Benoît's hurried departure had rather cooled her enthusiasm. So, the man, sensing her hesitation went immediately ahead:

"Safeguarding this object being my most cherished wish, miss, and as assured as I am that you will care for it with love and pass it on to future generations, I am ready to let you have it for a ridiculously low sum. Let us say, sixty dollars."

The transaction was rapidly concluded. All the more reason, since paying only sixty dollars for the chest, there would still be enough money for the rent. Benoît would thus be satisfied.

Mado marched off to take the subway with "Madam Corriveau's Chest" under her arm and the key at her neck, leaving behind her, on the surrounding terraces, a throng of young folks chattering, boozing, looking for a pickup or doing business.

Walking beneath the row of maples along her street, Mado

thought that she had really taken her little Treasure Seeker to the cleaners. But the pleasure of such a thought was of small duration. Indeed, upon arriving at home, she found there was little use in calling out and looking in all the rooms, Benoît wasn't there. After a few minutes, on the kitchen table, she found a short terse letter in Benoît's hand that staggered her:

Mado,
 This can't go on any longer. I've had enough of this kind of life. We'll never get anywhere this way. I'm off to spend a few days in the country, at my brother's place. After that, we'll see...
Benoît

Actually, Mado took the thing quite badly. She, first of all, phoned Black Lake, to contact Peter. This was Benoît's brother who, still knowing nothing about what was going on, showered her with insults.

Then, she went to sit on the back balcony, listening until eight o'clock to the children playing cowboys in the alley. And, at the hour when the mother's called their children in, she decided to go to bed.

Towards eleven, since she hadn't yet fallen asleep, she was watching the dark ceiling which seemed neither close nor far away. She was also thinking that it was quite idiotic to love a guy who was so scrupulous and upright!

Then, frazzled from sleeplessness, she decided to get up. It also came to her that a little sandwich made with sliced banana and peanut butter might make her feel better. Besides, didn't Benoît and herself often get up for a banana and peanut butter sandwich after having made love? She went back into the kitchen, more lonely now than when her insomnia was distressing her.

It was at that moment that she found herself once again face to face with the chest, that stupid chest that had brought all this about. Sparked by a gnawing anger, she threw it onto the floor, then gave it a kick. The chest rolled up against the wall, close to the floor lamp. A stream of light then struck the keyhole and glimmered in Mado's sleepy eyes.

Then her anger waned. She thought, and quite rightly so, that the story of the chest had merely provoked a further tear and that it was this tear that had caused the cup to overflow; it wasn't at all because the cup was already full. As a matter of fact, this incident had only been a deciding factor because of the position it occupied in relation to the ones before! Just as she now began to wonder, shortsighted as she had been for having bought "Madam Corriveau's Chest" without even opening it — and, in this, for the space of a second, she was ready to think Benoît had been right!

She hastened to search for the key that was hanging at her neck and easily found it still covering Benoît's pendant. She thought of him a moment as well, like a distant image, a hazy memory lurking in the fog. And bending over the chest, expecting to find nothing very extraordinary in what she now recognized to have been a rip-off, she gave further thought to her banana and peanut butter sandwich rather than the devilish trap, a trap that she herself was about to activate.

That night, Benoît couldn't sleep either. His brother, Pierre, had told him off quite soundly, reproaching him, as he had done Mado, for his lack of imagination, saying he showed no sense of humour or love of the world.

He was already disposed to accepting a good deal of the blame. He searched quite ardently within himself for explanations for his character and his conduct. He thought about his father, that forthright, just and highly respected man; his mother, playful, joke-loving but virtuous; his paternal grandfather, stern and deeply religious, and his grandmother, submissive and hard-working; of his maternal grandfather, more adventurous and really at ease only in society, and of his grandmother, a saintly woman ...

He also thought of his childhood (people always think of this when things go really wrong) a happy carefree period, given to uprightness and scholarly endeavour, spent with organized sports and the beginnings of television ...

He no longer knew if he had been right or wrong, and like all those caught between these extremes, he chose a middle-of-the-road approach. But that implied that Mado and he would both have to go half way.

All these arguments kept turning over and over in his head. It was only towards four in the morning that he finally came to understand that all this mental agitation was nothing more than the sign that he loved her.

Then, he quickly got dressed and, like a lover surprised at his love, he launched his Honda down the highway towards Montreal and his Mado.

When Benoît reached the Rosemont district, the sun was flashing in his rearview mirror at the top of Bellechasse Street. This brought him a bit back to reality. His dreams of perfect happiness didn't stand up in the light of day. What was more, sleepiness was beginning to gnaw away at his last efforts to watch the road. Now, the sun was hurting his eyes.

Rue St-Denis

As a matter of fact, Benoît was the victim of an off-peek period marked by low energy and lethargy which often, at sun up, shatters those unaccustomed to nightly activity. And so, he arrived home with his spirits weighed down and his body functioning at half speed.

Now, his pulse rate registered a serious and sudden quickening when he discovered that the apartment was empty. Mado wasn't there! Neither was the furniture nor his clothing, nor small daily articles such as his stamp collection, his pipe or his tools. Nothing, not even the blinds or curtains or carpets. Nothing at all remained except that damned chest, there, on the floor, near the wall!

Benoît couldn't believe his eyes! She had left, taking everything along with her. It was scarcely conceivable! He also considered that this justified his apprehensions and that he had done well in coming home that night.

However, as soon as this thought came to him, he wondered how she had been able to carry out this move as fast as she had! And he immediately concluded — and this reflection would have aroused the anger of many a woman — that another man must be involved. Thereupon, he let himself slip to the floor and his body gave way to sleep ... the sleep of the just.

It was the cries of children coming home from school that awoke him as well as the firmness of the floor about the level of his shoulder blades and at his rear end ; besides, there were his aches and a very stiff neck.

His first thought was for himself. He indeed wondered whether he was really going to wake up or fall back asleep, if reality would surpass his dreams or if the truth inside him was stronger than fiction. He was disappointed to realize that truth, dreams and fiction were all really the same thing, for the apartment had quite clearly been emptied!

He gazed all around in vain, nothing more now remained than a single object: the chest. There was only one solution— to depart as well.

Benoît then picked up the chest and left without even looking behind.

But what should he do? Where should he go? Scarcely was he aware of his solitude than it began to weigh quite heavily upon him! There was no one he was acquainted with who could put him up. No one, if not perhaps Émile, his inseparable companion at work. The highly gifted and easy-going Émile, that likable failure, that learned fellow polluted with alcohol and "pot" — his friend, Émile.

Benoît telephoned Émile but there was no answer. He tried the junior college; Émile had gone out to eat! And where would Émile drink and eat on a Friday if not on a terrace on rue Saint-Denis? So Benoît headed in that direction.

Chance, that abominable gift of both heaven and earth, led him to park his Honda close to the shop with the sign "The Treasure Seeker." Probably so as to respond to his unhappy fate and to take some revenge against that affected little man, Benoît, before going off to loaf about in the cafés in Émile's supportive company, made for this shop to return that useless chest.

To his great surprise, the little man received him warmly, inquiring about his health and the good spirits of his young female customer the night before.

Now, Benoît was waiting for nothing better than this. He who had been the butt of so much reproach let loose a stream of invective that informed the Treasure Seeker of everything that had happened. What is more, the latter — and Benoît noticed this only too clearly — gave a slight discreet smile, which was also rather mysterious and self-satisfied, for the man was aware that he had just found a treasure! Naturally, this smile sparked Benoît's anger.

However, the man behind the counter, anxious to put an end to this outburst and to retrieve his chest, offered to buy it back for fifty dollars.

Benoît's heart leapt.

"What! a chest that Mado payed a hundred dollars for only yesterday. How do you want me to get by with a hundred dollars? I've nothing any more. Neither clothes nor furniture nor anything ... "

The little man seemed even more pleased, but concealed his joy with a serious exterior, which was easier to do than the other way around, and he offered to give Benoît back the hundred dollars.

Surprised in turn, Benoît accepted the money and left abruptly without even saying goodbye and before the man could change his mind. But the thought also came to him that the Treasure Seeker really wasn't such a terrible fellow after all.

Once Benoît had gone, the man had immediately locked the door and drawn the store curtains. It hadn't even crossed his mind that he had lost forty dollars in the exchange.

He then telephoned right away to his most faithful customer who, until July first, was sojourning on one of the islands in the West Indies.

"Hello, fine sir," he said, catching the sound of the murmuring ocean, "I've a new chest for you. This time with a very pretty blond about twenty years old ... Yes, I'm sure you'll find her delightful ... Of course, dear sir, still the same price ... and by the usual route ... "

Then, feeling proud of his transaction, he had hung up and scurried off, rubbing his hands, to spend the rest of the day at a café speculating that one day his small savings would allow him to keep the girl ... just as, this time around, he had kept the furniture ...

CASIUS SAHBID'S FATALA

Sorcery, witchcraft and the arts of magic are also abolished by the very same statutes ordering that henceforth, no one whoever will be pursued for dabbling in spells, witchcraft, magic or sorcery.

*Justice of the Peace and Parish Officials,
for the Province of Quebec (1789)*

The air was chilly that evening on the islands off Man and his World. The docks of the marina at La Ronde were deserted as well. There was no one about, neither in the club nor on board the boats. Even Philippe Lacombe, who had frequented these docks every day since the beginning of spring, had decided to go and eat in a little restaurant on rue Saint-Denis, where he often used to take refuge at bad moments so as to reflect on this mysterious problem of successive murders.

The detective sergeant, Philippe Lacombe, Phil to his close friends, was involved in his first important investigation. Up to a point, it could be said that his future depended upon it. What is more, he didn't ignore the smallest clue nor neglect any approach whatever.

André Carpentier

After the meal, taking advantage the town being deserted, he had driven around the Saint-Louis district for some time, feeling home-sick and hankering after a few moments of distraction. In utter gloom, he roamed through these little streets that he loved so much and that he had so often scoured, on foot to begin with, then in a patrol car. However, this sombre story of murder along the dock area at La Ronde, which captivated public opinion at the same time it placed his career in jeopardy, was worrying him too much for him not to cast his stern shadow among the boats docked along the quays of the marina.

Approaching the docks, rather distraught in his thoughts and walking slowly in keeping with the chance directions of each step, he allowed himself to be gently guided towards the Fatala. As a matter of fact, it was close to this boat that four murders had taken place in a period of as many months.

Phil was deeply irritated by this story that seemed to have no conclusion. On the other hand, he thought he had checked out every lead, a thing that couldn't be accepted, since the murderer was still at large.

And perhaps for the hundredth time, Phil rehashed this dismal affair step by step.

First of all, there had been the recovery of the body of the first mate on board, a Greek, Nikos Markopoulos, on the twenty first of March last at two yards from the thirty-eight foot cruising ship: the Fatala. Then, all that futile investigation had followed. It must be said that Markopolous was already under suspicion, and rightfully so, it would seem, of smuggling without his boss, professor Casius Sahbid, knowing about it. There are cases where the police don't really try to search out and know the whole story — this was one of them. Markopoulos, a shameless adventurer whom Phil already knew not to be any saint was dead. One less of them. That was all.

Next, on the fifteenth of April, there was the strangling, as in the case of Markopoulos, of Magdala Sahbid, the daughter of professor Sahbid, owner of the Fatala. Then, a new fruitless investigation.

This time, Phil had been asked to make an exceptional effort. It concerned, after all, the daughter of an eminent professor! Oh, of course, Magdala wasn't considered to be any model of virtue! In Phil's eyes, at least, she wasn't any better than Markopoulos. What is more, that day, he saw her death as a kind of justice that had come about through injustice.

Then, on the twenty-seventh of May, they had fished out the body of Marc Langevin, who had also been strangled. Marc Langevin was the owner of the thirty-two foot cruising ship, the Chouan, moored beside the Fatala. At this point, Phil had investigated more strenuously the comings and goings of the second mate on board the Fatala: Igor Igor, a heavily built but gentle man with a bluish empty gaze and curly hair, as handsome as a Greek god who might have been believed in! Countryless, he travelled from one corner of the globe to the other taking jobs on boats and playing the harmonica.

Clearly, the case of Marc Langevin put the entire method of the investigation into question, for, this time, it was no longer the case of a foreigner. And Phil's superiors had indeed made him aware of the difference.

Finally, several days before, on the eighteenth, there had been the discovery of a fourth body just below the surface, again just a few yards from the Fatala. This time, it was Professor Sahbid himself, a Hindustani and owner of the Fatala, a boat flying an Indian flag. As well, the day after the fourth murder, that is to say, the night before last, Phil had put Igor Igor under arrest. However, things weren't easy with a man having no citizenship: the fellow defended himself well, and without really even trying.

It must be said as well that Phil wasn't really too convinced about Igor Igor's guilt; however, he had to arrest someone to persuade the press that the investigation was making headway and that the situation wasn't actually beyond him. All in all, he would have to admit that poor Philippe Lacombe of Émery Street, near Saint-Denis, had his hands full dealing with this affair, as weird, unique and morbid as it was! He kept discovering aspects to the case that were unsavoury and even shocking even though not related to his investigation. Besides this, their was the deeply enigmatic character of the people involved, along with their origins that were, how shall we say ... vague. Not to speak of this wave of superstition and mystery surrounding the whole business.

That evening in particular, he was feeling more disheartened than usual, probably due to the fear of making a mistake or of becoming over-anxious. However, he also had the feeling, deep down, that he was skirting the truth and circling around it without actually hitting upon it.

Now, here he was, approaching the celebrated cruising ship, the Fatala, moored to the wharf with two solid ... no, wait, a single hawser at the rear! This perception, right there and then, reminded him of one of the constant elements in all four cases: each time, in fact, he had found the boat secured by a single cable at the back while the front one was floating in the water. But how was it he hadn't noticed this before?

Tied up in this way, the front part of the Fatala had obviously nudged a certain distance away from the dock. Phil's reaction wasn't at all surprising, then, as he leaned unhesitatingly over the dirty water scanning its surface to see if perhaps another corpse wasn't waiting there for some cop to appear on the scene! However, under the circumstances, there was nothing abnormal bobbing about, merely an oil slick, two or three beer tins and a black bass that, lying there belly up, seemed to be cursing the human race.

All of this spread far and wide a sickly odour in the cold night and Phil thought that it would be better to depart, even though he was conscious that, this time, he hadn't come for nothing. However, before leaving, it seemed only rational to alert someone on board about this anomaly. He called out, the first few times with restraint, then shouting louder and louder. But even his last yells failed to elicit the slightest reply. To tell he truth, he really wasn't too surprised. Since the death of Casius Sahbib and his daughter, Magdala, no one was sure whom the boat belonged to. And the bow of this ship kept moving still farther and farther from the dock ...

Therefore, no doubt fearing the backwash, as well as his thoughts, while using a scrubbing brush left near the mooring post and grabbing onto the latter, Phil stretched out over the water and drew towards him the heavy hawser whose strand had unravelled a good yard at the end. At the same time, Phil, though little acquainted with the ethics and customs of the navy, was nonetheless rather astonished at this lack of proper maintenance. Although, since Sahbib's death, he once again ... No, he didn't spend too long thinking about this. Although it had become icy in the cold wind, he began pulling fiercely and steadily on the hawser so as to draw the front of the ship closer to the dock.

Once he had done this, he only had to tie the cable to the post.

At that very moment, he sensed that some absentmindedness on his part (or was it his usual clumsiness) had placed him in a rather painfully ludicrous situation. Indeed, the cable strands were weirdly wrapping themselves around his arms and clutching his shoulders! But this wasn't the worst of it; suddenly, the cable itself started to twist around his body, while the strands were invading his neck! Soon, he stopped struggling, leering scornfully at his grotesque plight ... . but then, he didn't laugh at all, for the cable was really getting a good grip! It was even growing tighter ...

It was then that Phil realized that the trail of Igor Igor had been a wrong one.

The cable and its ends were now snaring him even more vigorously; the vice was closing, and Phil, at that instant, lay there totally immobilized. Next, only his cries emerged from the pile of ropes ...

It goes without saying that Phil's long-limbed silhouette was no longer to be seen gliding discreetly between the tables and drinkers in the cafés on rue Saint-Denis, nor would his rather sad gaze be fixed upon the loving couples in restaurants and dance halls thereabout. For, at dawn, they will have fished his bluish body up from just below the surface near the cruising ship, the Fatala; the ship's loose mooring will, once again, have allowed the bow to float away from the quay.

Victorine's Flower Shop

I ruined myself in inexplicable bouts of despair.
Chateaubriand

The two men were riding down rue Saint-Denis in a black limousine, one of them sitting in the front wearing a navy cap and uniform with gold buttons, the other, sitting in the rear, holding onto a cigar and a briefcase.

Scarcely having turned off Metropolitan Boulevard which they had used to cross the island from west to east quite rapidly, the driver now had the impression he was stalling about, the traffic rhythm had slowed so much after they left the Boulevard. It appeared to be even more the case south of Rosemont and the tunnel. There, the cars assembled like a long snoring boa constrictor stretched out when it came to green lights and clumped together at the red ones.

The man with the cap fumed each time a dented missile skimmed by his shiny dark limousine, its slim chrome lines looking like tiny metal arrows set to slice through the heavy air on that humid late July afternoon. Since the man with the cigar liked him rather well after a good fifteen years of service, and since he had lain his newspaper aside, he launched into an extensive conversation with his chauffeur. Moreover, every time he had the chance, the man in the English tweed suit went about "sniffing" at the staff and taking the pulse of a model customer by discussing various questions with someone he considered virtually a friend.

"Where are we exactly?"

"On Saint-Denis, sir, near Sherbrooke."

There was something about this curt reply that brought to mind a problem that had haunted him over the last months ...

"Look there! Right by the plant shop of that crazy woman who finally died ... "

The chauffeur was quick to agree, but he couldn't help adding, as though reproachfully:

"Once again you've won, sir."

The man in the back holding his briefcase pretentiously on his knees noticed his chauffeur's accusing tone; what is more, he attempted to vindicate his actions claiming that he urgently needed this building since he wanted to establish an immense outdoor restaurant there.

"I was already the owner of the houses on each side for some three years and this one for nearly two years. And for two years I have never been able to get my project underway because of her, that crazy old witch! Every time I tried to get her out, she thwarted me with her manoeuvres."

While the neck and legs of the man with the cap were getting redder and redder, the one in the rear seat recalled the time when, having sent some strong arm types to the place, he had found them in the alley more dead than alive; another time, his lawyer had appeared in court in a pair of Bermuda shorts with a bag of candies in his hand, looking more like a child than a grown up; then, there was the occasion when he had attempted, as a last resort, to have the witch's shop set on fire; the professional arsonist hired for the job had come back looking more drowned than singed! As he was relating all this to his brave friend in the cap perhaps for the tenth time, he spotted the much talked of shop and its wood and wrought-iron sign:

VICTORINE'S FLOWER SHOP

He also noticed, as did others, that the window was covered with soap streaks and the door boarded up. This, once again, reminded him that he had long dreamed of removing the shroud surrounding the magician's den. And so, in a rather bullheaded way, he asked his chauffeur to park the car as soon as possible; thereupon, the latter reacted so promptly that the man with the briefcase wondered if there wasn't something magical about this as well.

Then, the two men, after having dragged themselves out of the car, headed slowly towards the flower shop.

While passers-by, feigning disinterest, were eying the man with the briefcase who was pulling the door, trying to glimpse inside, the man with the cap, as though he were rooted to the spot, wavered between his means of livelihood and his loving heart; he was wondering if the security offered by his chauffeur's job was really as important to him as had been his blind loyalty throughout the years to this witch ; at the same time, he suspected that he may have been merely a gullible instrument, an unthinking handy man seconding a manufacturer of strange concoctions. He thought as well of the numerous people who had disappeared, the sick, injured or deranged ones who had attempted to oppose the evil powers of the apparently young, yet old, Victorine.

Still standing quite still behind the master he served with his cap under his arm, he was obliged to shake himself free of these thoughts when a neighbour, a bookstore clerk, appeared to recognize him:

"You're the man in the red shirt! The one who helped Victorine for such a time, who often crept by the walls in our alley, at night, carrying strange packages, who got in the way when we were about to level with her ... "

The man with the cap didn't flinch nor did he turn red while calmly facing the accusations of the little man who was fired up with anger and a desire for revenge..

In any case, it was the man with the briefcase who appeared at first to defend his chauffeur, or perhaps it was only to look into his integrity.

"Come now! What are you babbling about there, sir. Our good friend here wouldn't hurt a fly!"

Scarlet in the face, the little man defiantly stepped up and fired in the face of his adversary:

"It has nothing to do with flies, sir, but it concerns men, women and children who have been tortured, broken and destroyed by spells, potions and infusions ... and I can certify that this fellow was involved."

He allowed a few moments to go by, time enough for his words to sink in, and, turning towards the man with the cap, urged on now by some passers by, he said in a voice that was both calm and dramatic — much like a book salesman who catches a young college student shoplifting:

"Sir, if you are so entirely innocent, why don't you let us search you?"

Hardly had these words been spoken than two men from the district seized the chauffeur by the shoulders and the little clerk offered to let the man with the briefcase frisk his companion himself; this the latter did after hesitating a few seconds, cautiously, laying his case down close by.

He excused himself, first of all, to his friend for having to go about this search which was quite embarrassing for both of them, then he went on with it starting with the jacket pockets, wondering himself all the while whether, by doing this, he was actually trying to find the man in navy blue guilty or innocent.

He first discovered a set of keys; the shouts of the crowd rose louder and louder:

"The keys to the witch's shop!"

Somebody grabbed them immediately and ran off to try them in the front and back doors of the store.

When, to the great disappointment of the crowd, the fellow came back with the news that they didn't work, the chauffeur's jacket had been removed and his pant pockets gone through. The more the search progressed the more the man in navy-blue could see the moment pending when when they would have proof of his guilt. He sensed, furthermore, that he had already been exposed and recognized as one of Victorine's numerous secret accomplices! And it was with an air of defeat that, when someone asked whether the keys were not those of some other clandestine meeting place or of the witch's apartment, he blurted, with his eyes turned towards the shop:

"Victorine only lived here. She never left this place ... "

Right away, the murmurs of the crowd changed to threats and insults. Conscious of what his words implied, several tried to get at him. They kicked at him or tried to punch him in the head ... they grabbed at his shirt! ... then and there, there were more and more traces of his guilt.

To begin with, a scar on his left arm was now visible which made the old landlady on the corner almost strangle with rage, for she recognized the mark of a red-hot poker that she had administered to a man of the same stocky figure, wearing a sizeable redshirt, his face shrouded by a nylon stocking, who had come to carry off her poor husband's corpse; he had suddenly passed away after having drunk one of the witch's concoctions!

Next, before the crowd could react to this absolutely inane story, the little clerk, pulling open the white shirt of the witch's accomplice, exposed a tiny bag of herbs hanging at his neck; this concealed an alchemist design, clearly etched on his chest, representing a crucible crowned with rare herbs and Latin names. Many others present were enraged victims driven on as well by a overpowering desire for revenge after the disappearance of the lovely Miss Gertrude, (a cashier in the same bookstore as himself until her disappearance the year before). Once again, a spontaneous thunderous uproar broke out from the crowd.
"Let him eat his own herbs!"
The shouting on all sides would surely have impressed any newcomer.
"Let's hang him from the shop's sign!"
Next, things began to move very fast.
Just as some of them were beginning to tear away the planks that boarded up the entrance way, there came the sound of sirens. Everybody realized that it was really too late to take justice into their own hands. They all understood instinctively, as well, that they would be let go scot free for having given in to their bitterness and for burning down the witch's headquarters.
In the scramble that followed, the door and window were quickly smashed in exposing a tangled mass of philodendrons, asparagus, spider lilies, begonias and cactuses, their wild intrusive appearance forcing the throng to step back a pace.

Then, the man with the briefcase, who had shrewdly drawn away from the more agitated group for the last several minutes, rushed forward shoving those around him and shouting for the whole place to be destroyed. Urged on by his cries, by the uproar of the crowd that was even holding up traffic on rue Saint-Denis, and by the deafening scream of the sirens close by, the most aggressive types dashed inside the shop yelling: "Let's set fire to it!"

Next, they plunged into the store, some with lighters, some carrying paper that was already aflame.

The crowd then rushed towards the door and the window. However, as the first of these reached the shop, they made a violent effort to pull back, thus keeping other onlookers at a reasonable distance from the dramatic scene. For it was indeed dramatic.

In point of fact, through the window and doorway, they all could see the perfectly white stiffened bodies of the few most daring ones who had attempted to set fire to the witch's lair. All of these bodies, woven among the multiple stems of the plants and partially covered by their leaves, dangled there menacingly on display, looking much like the corpses of hanged men at the entrances to pioneer towns in the American wild West!

Silence then fell over the awe-struck crowd. No one could believe his eyes: was this really caused by the power of the plants? Had there been some magical intervention? Had Victorine dealt another blow to that spirited race of inoffensive bystanders, those who had nothing to reproach themselves for since, due to circumstance, they had always kept away from occasions for breaking the law?

At that moment, the crowd, although stunned and still thirsting for vengeance, turned its rancour against the spellbound chauffeur still loyal to his witch. The latter stood tightly gripped by the little book salesman and the man with the briefcase. And, of course, this zeal didn't go unheeded.

While the first policemen were rushing to the scene, the excited crowd shouted fiercely at the accomplice of the bewitched madwoman, but also at the book salesman responsible for this near riot and the man with the briefcase who — though unaware of doing so — had for such a time supported this accomplice; this mob, then, let go all its fury, jostling the three men and finally shoving them forcibly into the dark shop with its tangle of plants!

Next, in the crush, a policeman and a slightly drunken bystander were also propelled inside.

Some hurled paper and flaming cardboard through the window. Another, who was more daring, pulled down the wrought-iron framed wooden sign, set fire to it and hurled it through the window; the scene, with the bits of glass forming a frame around the plants and corpses of the first bold attackers, reminded onlookers of a movie screen onto which an old Tarzan adventure was being projected.

This was followed by a loud cry, a kind of long shrill screech that made everyone freeze on the spot. No one moved or spoke. The fire spread while no one dared approach, completely stunned as they were by the prolonged wail!

And so, the shop burned, for hours and hours it burned away all by itself! In fact, to the great surprise of all those who thronged the scene of the disaster, the fire spread neither to the neighbouring houses nor even to the rest of the building! It lasted the entire night with the firemen's hoses being of little use to stop it.

For all this time, as well, the long shrill wail continued, breaking off only in the morning at the same time the fire finally burned out.

When the first firemen finally decided to enter Victorine's Flower Shop, just at that hour when the traffic on Saint-Denis was beginning to intensify, one body was missing, the body of the man in the navy-blue uniform with gold buttons.

Ogda's Double

> *There's so many places where you ain't
> it's as though I was swimming in your presence.*
>
> Michel Garneau

The principal character in this story bears the hundred thousand names of God; we will also call him simply: God ...

God, and this was indeed the case before we ever conceived of writing this tale, lived peacefully in his Paradise; to simplify matters, we will just say that He was living with a woman, a woman whose name was never passed on to us by tradition. We will merely call her Ogda.

Now, one day, this being the situation, Ogda suddenly fell ill, struck down by an illness so strange and disturbing it had to be recognized even by God! Ogda was dying; and apparently, God couldn't do anything about it! There was something more godly than He at the bottom of all this! Indeed, neither science nor prayers were of any avail.

And God, if we are to believe what we are told by word of mouth, loved Ogda more than anything. But hours growing into weeks, months into years, centuries into seconds, or whatever all this entails, he could do nothing but watch the steady advance of the malady. Ogda was failing; what is more, her condition was leaving its mark on the immediate environment, growing worse and worse until the end, that is to say, when all is said and done, Ogda's end.

There then! Ogda was dead. In that infinity in which everything fades away and everything is created, Ogda was no longer any more than a memory in God's mind, but a very gripping memory — indeed, we have to say, a very intense one.

So, God ordered an end to all feasts and festivities, fireworks, fountains and hanging gardens ... God was alone and Paradise quite empty ...

And so time passed until the day when God, who holds the secret of life, neither capable nor desirous of freeing Himself of Ogda's memory, set about creating her double. He began timidly, tentatively, by designing a male creature whom He called Adam, then, becoming more audacious, He attempted right off to make an Ogda. The result wasn't really a bad one but this young woman, the product of some of Adam's surplus features, only vaguely resembled his own Ogda. Besides this, it must be said, she was more interested in Adam than she was in God. Therefore, both disappointed by his semi-defeat and, indeed, jealous of Adam and Eve's idyll, He flew into a memorable rage and stuck the indecent couple in a cosmic incubator which He named "the universe" before placing it in isolation.

He was hoping that, in this way, through reproduction, from generation to generation, He would one day find Ogda's double in the incubator! Then, He would take this double back with Him and restore life to his Paradise lost ...

Rue St-Denis

This has all been going on for hundreds of millions of years, and God hasn't yet seen Ogda through his sacred circular window. He appears to be keeping the faith, but He's actually close to despair. Adam and Eve, of course, no longer exist. However, as planned, they have engendered innumerable descendants. And there's the problem: how can He keep an eye out for everyone of them ... or rather, for all of the females? For God, this is all quite discouraging and He only observes his incubator in his idle moments. Moreover, his calculations covering different probabilities being probably not too sure, up until now He has only seen imperfect doubles, or blemished ones! For only the physical angle counts in so far as God is concerned ...

Elvira, sweet Elvira, the lover and concubine of the famous cyclist, Patam Starrick, is ill, gravely ill ...

Though it be to his loss, Patam can do nothing about it. Patam loves his Elvira more than anything and he attempts a last effort besides. This morning, Patam has accompanied Elvira to a doctor on rue Saint-Denis who is well known for his clear-cut diagnoses. We are indeed referring to a scholar, professor Deaddome who, highly qualified in observing the rapid advancement of a disease, prescribes courage, self-denial and prayers, before during and after meals!

"A question of weeks," he told them, "a mere question of weeks ... " Elvire and Patam repeat these four words over and over again as they leave the office of this great specialist in death. The phrase rings in their heads as they breach the air on rue Saint-Denis, she sitting on the handlebars and he on the seat of his machine, his neck stretched to the right so that he might see where he's going.

Without agreeing on it or being aware they are doing so,

they both ask God, though they no longer know how to pray, to call Elvira back as quickly as possible, since neither of them has the makeup to endure situations *in extremis*.

The reader will have imagined — he being, after all, well-read — that this is the precise moment God chooses to cast a neglectfully divine glance inside his incubator, towards Montreal and down Sherbrooke and rue Saint-Denis. It 's also at this very moment he observes the purest double of his Ogda that he had seen in a million years. This double, of course, is Elvira riding on Patam's ten speed. So God, now impatient and rather tense, without checking more closely and refusing to find any more discreet occasion, draws Elvira-Ogda away to himself!

As things go, this results purely and simply in the disappearance of Elvira from Patam's handlebars, who right there and then, loses his leather helmet! Elvira, his charming Elvira, so splendid and so lusty, is no longer there. A second before, she was and suddenly, without forewarning and for no apparent reason if it isn't for the granting of their prayers, Elvira is replaced by empty space! Patam, must we tell you, crashes on his right side and scrapes his face on the edge of the sidewalk along rue Saint-Denis a mere turn or two of his wheels from the corner of Ontario. There's little need to say as well that he will remain marked by this event till the end of his days.

Elvira-Ogda is lying motionless on the ground beside the incubator. God, bending over her, thanks his great beyond. His lips tremble and He murmurs:

"Who would have thought it?"

Cautiously and gently, He takes her in his divine arms and leads her to his Paradise on the slopes where their first love took place, but it is of little avail for Him to speak of tenderness, Elvira-

Ogda is still unconscious.

Then, rather disturbed by this (as we might well imagine) God decides to go and fetch some salts and a clothe dampened with cold water. Before coming back out, however, feeling quite perky (we can understand that too), He starts up the mechanism for the fountains, orders that the gardens should be suspended once again and that midnight is to be proclaimed with gigantic fireworks accompanied by great feasts. Next, after a brief affectionate glance for which there is just enough time to thank Him, He shuts down the cosmic incubator!

Then, He sets off to rejoin his Elvira-Ogda who, on the tiny slope, as God will come to realize too late for the rest of us, expires murmuring: "Patam, your wheel is spinning ... "

André Carpentier

The Beyond-Time Bookshop

No man can bear the uncovering of his motives.
Fries, Fries, Fries
Arnold Wesker

At age 35, Luc Guindon was a young writer highly esteemed in literary circles. Moreover, his first three novels had received a momentous welcome from the public. It must be said that these three works, their plots reflecting the very heart of 19th century French-speaking Montreal, appeared in a "retro" style that was then highly in vogue. However, for Luc Guindon, this wasn't the result of a mere fad, but it stemmed rather from a passion that his undertakings as a chronicler justified and facilitated. For Luc was known above all as a historiographer, a specialist in the slender history of the town of Montreal and its general area. Furthermore, his two works, *The Short History of "the Main"* and *A History of the Districts of Montreal*, had known great success in bookstores, bringing him a few prizes from nationalist sectors as well as the admiration of that generation of junior college students whose professors had made them read these two volumes.

For his living, Luc ran a history chronicle about the city of

Montreal on the air waves of FM Radio-Canada (for everyone knows that royalties bring authors scarcely enough bread for them to dunk in their soup).

What is more, Luc Guindon was also known as the son of the famous notary, Armand Guindon, who was at one and the same time, alderman under Camille Houde, a silent deputy under Duplessis and as himself, a historian and specialist on a brief history of the city of Montreal. Guindon, the notary, died in 1972 at seventy-seven years of age.

However, Luc was known above all as the grandson of Lucien Guindon (1845-1923), literary and music critic at *La Minerve* and then at *La Presse* and as a famous prophetic writer towards the end of the Nineteenth Century — as a matter of fact, the only science-fiction writer in our literary history. And what a genius he was in his prognoses, discerning well before their time the upsurge of some of the greatest technical innovations of the Twentieth Century. Atomic power, for example, which he already discussed in 1879 in a short story called "Three hours later"; the skyscraper whose social role he described quite closely as soon as 1881 in another short story named "Suddenly there was a lack of air"; or small scale electronics in "Voyage to the centre of the moon" (1884). One might also mention a number of scientific, medical and even artistic inventions in our century which, in his time, brought upon him odious marks of ridicule and general derision at the hands of Montreal and Quebec's right-minded French-speaking society, with, at the forefront, the clergy and some troubled intellectuals of that period.

And so, it is only now, more than fifty years after his death, that this great visionary is being rediscovered! And this thanks to a remarkably well documented work written and published at the author's expense by his grandson, Luc Guindon. Following the immense success of this book, entitled *Lucien Guindon, Visionary*,

Luc had already re-edited more than thirty of the almost two hundred and twenty-five short stories written by his precursor between 1878 and 1899.

Luc was satisfied to a certain extent with his style of living. Although his income didn't leave too much room for fanciful pastimes, he was lucky enough to be able to approach his work following his own tastes and at his own speed (an advantage he was quite aware of). For example, he fostered a voluminous correspondence with numerous historians or, quite simply, with elderly people who were able to attest to various facts concerning our short history which upheld the originality of his documentation.

Now, that very morning, upon leaving his home, Luc had met his friend, Ti-Bi, the postman, whom he considered as one of his chief intermediaries. Ti-Bi had handed him a letter (a single letter, and this he found surprising) which he began to read while walking down good old Laval Street in the direction of Saint-Louis Square. But such a letter could only arrive all by itself, or so he thought as he advanced further into reading this strange missive:

Montreal, August 16, 1978

Dear Sir,

I am an elderly man (in fact, I will soon be ninety years old), who knew your grandfather quite well during the last years of his life; I mean the now finally famous Lucien Guindon.

Lucien Guindon was a very withdrawn and bitter man. And this bitterness, caused by the lack of understanding he endured from intellectuals of his time, made him into a man very little given to words, to such a point that it was impossible for his friends and myself, we who admired him so greatly, to bring him to reveal the real reasons that led him to his laterday career as a science-fiction writer.

Never did he agree to reveal to us this 'momentous secret' he sometimes alluded to which lay, if we are to believe his last words, at the roots of his astonishing career.

If I take it upon myself to write to you today, it is to point out a small error which has slipped into that very fine and very interesting study that you have just devoted to him.

In effect, you state on page 97 that, in his work, he never mentioned his own time but that the action in his short stories always takes place at, what is for us, the present, that is to say, his own future. In this, you are virtually correct... I say virtually, for there are three exceptions to this rule: three exceptions that can be reduced, moreover, to a single one for it concerns three short stories ("The clock in the desert", "The End of the ice" and "The Wireless image") all of which begin in the same way. The hero, at the beginning of each one of these tales, in fact, visits a bookseller who has a shop on rue Saint-Denis in order to ask his advice...

Mister Guindon, I ask you to believe me, this bookseller was my father, Antoine, who was a close friend of Lucien Guindon and, as a result, he often received him in our home and at his shop under the sign, The Beyond-Time Book Shop. I myself often hopped onto your grandfather's knees before becoming your father's friend, myself being seven years his senior and as well, by heaven, the confident of your grandfather towards the end of his life.

I would very much like to meet you and to speak with you of those times... I have so many things to tell you.

Come around five o'clock, but don't be too late, for at my age...

Hector Dumas
xxxx, rue Saint-Denis
Montreal

ANDRÉ CARPENTIER

For the first time, since he had moved into this district which he loved so much, Luc strolled, as he had the habit of doing, through Saint-Louis Square, without thinking about everything this park represented for numerous generations of Francophones; nor did he seek to catch the eye of some girls from one of Old Montreal's junior colleges who often came to sit there attracted by the trees, the warm breeze and the chirping of local birds. He walked straight towards rue Saint-Denis kicking himself for not having discovered this extraordinary witness to the last years of Lucien Guindon's life before he had published his book!

Then, suddenly, as though jolted back to reality by the position of the sun, he observed that it was only noon hour. He had still five hours to put in before going to have a chat with Hector Dumas. This left him ample time to go to the National Library to pick up a bit of information on the Beyond-Time Bookshop so as, of course, to make his conversation with the old man that much easier. But he was soon to be disappointed ...

In the beginning, his research met a dead end. However, in some old annuals, he did learn that this bookshop had existed, but only between 1878 and 1899! An astonishing fact since this period covered quite clearly the duration of the prophetic writer, Lucien Guindon's career. Luc hadn't worked on those twenty-one years and some months for this coincidence not to spring immediately to his attention. He strode out of the National Library more anxious than ever to meet Hector Dumas. However. since it was still only ten past two, he went and sat on a terrace and drank a few beers among an animated group, eying some and chatting with others. The weather in Montreal was torrid on that August day and the humidity swamped everything in its passage, which made him speak more emphatically than usual and drink even more heavily, continually wiping his moustache with the back of his sleeve and exhaling often down the neck of his white shirt.

He put in the time this way, passing from one glass to another, one girl to another and from one group of friends to another, all of them feeling quite parched while they sank into endless and perfectly sterile conversations. This all took place so swiftly that it was only when hearing someone order food that he realized that it was after five! His stupefaction increased tenfold when he noticed a few steps away, in rue Saint-Denis, that it was already night time! The dark appeared to be impenetrable; only a few bright windows gave the impression that there was life beyond his café. You might have thought it was all an immense instrument panel indicating the details of a flight beyond the shadows of time.

And so, Luc had muffed his rendezvous. He was probably even too late to go and knock on the old man's door who, in any case, must already have been sleeping for some time, comfortably bathed in some images out of his past. And then, even if he wasn't drunk enough to notice it, he was certainly too much that way to take the chance of ruining such an important meeting!

The only thing he could do was to start drinking again. And the more he drank, the more he kept thinking that the night was no more than some feeble ephemeral link between boundless generative sources of sunshine and life. This all lasted until the ground began to sway beneath his feet and his tongue stumbled over difficult syllables. Then, urged by those around him who had had to listen, he decided to go home and rest his turbulent brain on a stack of pillows ...

However, this didn't take into consideration the strange hazards and troublesome mysteries of the darkness of night ... that moonless, halo-less darkness that makes the night birds flip about in the black shadows ...

André Carpentier

Now, often in the evening, in streets the style of great cities, flocks of distraught souls come with their owlish figures to amble around in one another's tracks and, so as to distinguish themselves from the agitated strollers of the day, these night-birds, usually in small groups confusing the sun and moon, punctuate the shadows with their mournful stride and tread in the chiaroscuro of ill-lit streets. Often also, resembling a jumble of hooks loaded with old coats crisscrossing the night, they pass by one another without the slightest sign of recognition ... since, as Luc would say, in the night, all birds are grey!

Upon vacating the terrace of the café, that evening, he had the impression he belonged body and soul to this pale stooped race which he had always regarded in an absentminded way without, of course, realizing that he too belonged to this same breed as fruit does to its tree. This he found somehow reassuring and he now felt at home in this scattered though hearty nightly throng. He smiled towards unknown passersby and felt rather proud of it. If he only could have kept walking straight, instead of staggering and zigzagging, he would have been quite content.

He concentrated all his energies, then, in maintaining his moral and physical balance. And it was no doubt with this goal in mind that he suddenly began to read systematically all the addresses of houses that he was laboriously ambling by. He went on reciting the numbers aloud, then began answering his own echo. Next, he began running so as to sustain the rhythm of his own reading. But, as it often happens, since the body doesn't always obey the mind, he tumbled heavily onto the sidewalk after having tangled his feet in a typically Chaplinesque manoeuvre. As expected — and as it usually happens with drunks — he wasn't hurt. His head slammed violently against a fire hydrant, though he apparently wasn't aware of doing so.

In point of fact, rather than pain, it was his solitude, his sense of loneliness in this usually congested street that left him quite perplexed. It appeared to him, feeling as lost as he did, that he was suspended in both space and time, and that a moon beam, like a stage reflector lighting up but him alone, shone forth so as to isolate him on some immense stage. However, it wasn't the moon — that poor loony lady gone off to sweep through the daylight that englobes it in its rays — it was a store window which he perceived at an angle with its interior lighting shining brighter and brighter. Through this window he could also make out, with growing clarity, the presence of a man about thirty years of age, with a wide beard and reddish hair, who appeared to be busy perusing old newspapers.

Forcing his eyes to assume a detached gaze, Luc was able to read, painted in a half-circle in the window:

THE BEYOND-TIME BOOKSHOP

This appeared to sober him up quite sharply! Then, he got back up and slowly crept towards this unknown bookstore, like a hunter seeking his prey ... He at first thought that this was the only bookstore which he wasn't acquainted with in Montreal and the general area. And besides this, it was so close by and in this very rue Saint-Denis that he thought he knew by heart!

Then, he read twice over again the name of the shop both inside the window as well as on the wrought-iron sign visible only in the exterior lighting. He also yanked Hector Dumas' letter from his pocket to make himself fully aware of the fact that he was at the very same address!

No doubt about it, he was now quite carried away with curiosity and so, feeling thoroughly inept before such a mystery, as are all great seekers of the truth, he decided to knock on the door of the Beyond-Time Bookshop.

Strangely enough, the red-haired man who answered seemed to recognize him even through the glazed window. What is more, he received Luc with such deference that the latter considered him to be rather pompous and affected.

"What an honour for me, dear Mister Guindon, to welcome you to my humble shop ... and all the more so since its official opening isn't until tomorrow!"

"Then, I'll be a harbinger of good things," Luc replied, highly excited.

"Let us hope it will endure a hundred years or even longer."

Thereupon, the two men went on quite a good bit with smiling, bowing and scraping until the bookstore manager, with a classy wave of the hand as well as a twist of his gaze showing the way, allowed his visitor to pass between the bookshelves so he might hunt about for books.

Then, there began for Luc an astonishing tryst with knowledge and pleasure. Astonishing, because the young historiographer, for some reason he wasn't too sure of himself, didn't really feel at ease, even though, upon first impressions, it would seem he was truly in his element. Moreover, to start with, he merely looked about without touching a thing, like some shy guest who first waits for his host to serve himself some chips or a sandwich.

This moment of hesitation, which was more physical than mental, allowed him to come to terms quite rapidly with his confusion. And so he was able to make out the cause of this unease in bookish surroundings which was unusual for him: it was the time frame! That is to say the period all these books covered: from the end of the Eighteenth to the beginning of the Nineteenth Century!

And at the very moment he became aware of this, he heard

the red-headed dealer behind him, while leaning over a chest, applaud in a most ingratiating way upon seeing what it contained. So Luc, much like the shy guest before a tray of sandwiches who unwittingly picks on the most appetizing one, pulled out a large leather-bound volume.

This beautiful object, as was truly the case, brought him for a brief second a deep feeling of comfort mingled with a sense of novelty and sophistication. On the cover, two small initials, A. D., engraved in the very middle gave a golden lustre to the dark leather.

As well, this curious book was composed of some thirty blank pages protected by an equal number of onion skin sheets, the majority of which bore sketches in bright colours. What is more, these sketches, which were no doubt originals, all represented the same building, sometimes viewed from the outside, sometimes showing the interior. The words "The Beyond-Time Bookshop, original drawings by A.D., copy number twenty-one," written with a style no longer seen in our day, could also be read on a fly leaf.

"Tell me," Luc nervously blurted at the red-headed man who, quite absorbed in his work, gave a start at the sound of his customer's voice, "Is this book for sale?"

"Of course," the other replied, approaching him, "since it's on the bookshelves. But I fear it's rather expensive. You see, I did those sketches myself, one by one and ... "

"How much?" Luc interjected, astonished by the bookseller's demeanour.

However, the fellow hesitated, not knowing too well how to go about all this, which was something Luc did not fail to notice. So he decided to play the role of a very casual customer.

"You wouldn't sell it for fifty dollars ... "

"Certainly not," the red head replied. "But for less than forty dollars, I don't know whether ... "

Luc was flabbergasted, this book was worth several times that sum! So he asked about the prices of some other rare volumes visible in the shelves and in a small windowed book case. There was no doubt whatever that the prices given by the bookseller were really far too low! About ten or fifteen percent of their true value!

Fearing then that these collector's items might fall into the hands of the unschooled, Luc decided to forewarn the young man of just how unrealistic his prices were but not without first having taken advantage of the situation. Then, although he was rather shaky thanks to the feelings of stress that assailed him, he managed to stack into a wooden case about forty books having a total price of one hundred and five dollars and asked that the whole thing be put aside.

"I'll come tomorrow with the money."

However, suddenly remembering that he was to spend the entire next day in a studio taping a special series devoted to the history of the Hochelaga district, he informed the bearded young man that a major difficulty prevented him from returning the next day before closing hours.

"No matter," replied the bookseller,"I'll wait for you until seven o'clock. Look, here's your bill."

And the two men took leave of one another, both feeling they had made a good bargain.

In the muffled hubbub of the sleeping masses through which History regenerates its various links, it is difficult to make out what actually happened to the young book salesman, whereas, in Luc's case, he rushed off to spend the rest of the night in a sombre disco on Saint Lawrence Street. Of the horrid night that followed he recalled only the oppressive images of beer, music and the flashing of coloured lights, all of this combined with a violent headache which began hammering in his brain at sunrise.

Then it was that, even more subtly, like some tenacious memory, the noise of a horse galloping along the pavement came back to him along with the echoing clatter of several carriages disturbing the silence of the sleeping city ...

The next day, towards six o'clock, tiptoeing out of the studios of Radio-Canada so as not to further aggravate his headache, Luc headed directly towards rue Saint-Denis and the Beyond-Time Bookshop.

If at first he found he had been inattentive in not marking the store's exact location, next he felt rather inept at not discovering the place right away. In the end, he was swayed by a sense of stupidity at not finding it at all.

He consulted Hector Dumas' letter to make sure that he was actually in front of the address in question, that is to say, theoretically speaking, the Bookshop itself. But nothing was to be found there than a rooming house much as they are to be discovered so plentifully on rue Saint-Denis. No bookstore or red-headed manager!

Having then nothing at all to lose, he walked inside to ask the landlady for information. However, when he mentioned the Bookshop he was supposed to have visited the night before, the stout lady took advantage of the occasion to advise him to give up drink and to devote himself to a life of faith and prayer. When he asked if she knew of an old gentleman responding to the name of Hector Dumas, she informed him that the old man had died the night before, that the dead man's son, whose address and first name she was unaware of, had taken everything away and that the room was already occupied by a young ballerina from Jonquière.

Luc felt a bit ill. He couldn't understand at all what was happening. He cut short all the prattle, which succeeded in making the landlady angry, and went off to stroll around Saint-Louis Square, then, a bit further north, where the antique dealers are found.

However, before leaving, he crossed the street so as to stand away from the situation for a moment, just to see if perhaps he hadn't chosen the wrong house. After all, this bookstore couldn't just, in a few hours, have disappeared into thin air! Unless, in the course of his boozing the evening before, he had been in another street, which was scarcely probable ... or else ... or else he had merely dreamed the whole story! Was he beginning to confuse the real with the imaginary, was he inventing all this? Was he losing his mind?

As though he were trying to wipe this last possibility out of his thoughts, he shook his head and shouted aloud:

"But where is it?"

Scarcely had he done this than a tall man in a uniform came up to ask him, with much authority, what he had lost.

"The bookstore! The Beyond-Time Bookshop ... "

The policeman looked dark.

"Are you sure you didn't get the wrong street?"

"Am I sure? It was here last night ... "

For the second time in a few minutes, Luc was advised to give up drinking ... above all before meals! His ears also caught the word "druggie" and this at least made him laugh a bit.

Later, wandering from the window of one antique shop to another, while complying with those who encouraged abstinence, Luc wondered once again if, upon striking his head on the ground and against the fire hydrant, his brain hadn't quite simply begun to flip about, bringing to the fore a certain number of suppressed desires, as well as a few of his more daring dreams as a collector!

However, a tiny act on his part wiped away this possibility.

Rue St-Denis

Putting his hand in his jacket pocket, he indeed found the yellowish bill bearing the effigy of the Beyond-Time Bookshop with a total cost of one hundred and five dollars! Moreover, the address was identical with the one written on the letter of the late Hector Dumas.

Nevertheless, a tiny detail on this bill suddenly gave him over to some very troublesome food for thought! The date: August 18, 1878!

During the days that followed, Luc saw his mail pile up at an alarming rate: some of the research he had been working on also lay on the corner of his desk without his giving it the slightest attention. He neglected as well his weekly chronicle, being satisfied to speak about generalities and warmed over material, paraphrasing some and quoting others, although all this wasn't very usual for him.

Every evening, as well, he plodded down rue Saint-Denis as far as the cafés and terraces and returned home after closing hours, generally quite drunk, but with a very dry throat besides for having talked so much. And when he would walk by the location of the celebrated phantom bookstore, even when he was with friends, he would always stop for a few seconds, much as though he still entertained the hope of finding some trace of the shop and the red-haired man!

Now, one evening when it was raining and the wind was blowing fiercely, — it may have been around twelve thirty — at the very moment he was slowly tramping along against the storm — shivering and chilled to the bone, how great must have been his surprise, or it might be said, virtually his horror upon raising his eyes absent-mindedly towards Hector Dumas' former rooming house, only to discover the Beyond-Time Bookshop, gently reflecting a glimmering diffused light. It came back to him that it had looked this way the very first time ...

He marched headlong towards it, this time more intent upon seeking his own mental equilibrium than in hunting for collector's items. Besides this, it should be remembered that he had long since spent, or should we say, guzzled down the one hundred and five dollars that he had gone to fetch at the Caisse populaire, the day following his first visit to the Bookshop.

So his first reaction was to rush up to the the red-haired man and ask him to assure him that this was his business address. However, he scarcely had the time to utter his first words than the salesman, adopting an overbearing tone, began upbraiding him severely for his tardy arrival!

Luc wasn't too clear as to what was happening. He stammered that he was aware of all this ... . that he was quite sorry, but that ... he just couldn't say what he meant; the other man went on scolding him quite spitefully. And while he was bending over the counter to pull out the case Luc had put aside, he banged heavily into the young historian while uttering a phrase which was, for him, unusually trite.

"I told you yesterday that I would wait for you until about seven o'clock, Mister Guindon. May I point out that it is now nearly one in the morning. It is surely because of the admiration that I have for you and for the work that you do that ... "

"Yesterday," Luc blurted out, totally taken aback!

"Yes ... yesterday evening ... when you came here ... "

At that moment, things began to move very fast for Luc.

While he was attempting to explain to the man that the scene he was referring to had taken place some ten days before, a noise that was both startling and familiar diverted his attention. They were the sounds of another time — a carriage clattering in tune with the energetic galloping of a horse and this accompanied by the oil lamps dancing on the counter and the bottom shelf, mingled as well with the romantic bearing of the red-haired fellow, all of which opened his eyes as to the real significance of the events of the days preceding this moment.

However, he pretended not to understand; this was all impossible, not to say, unthinkable! How could he, after all, have returned in time to the period of his dear ancestor, the mysterious but ageless Lucien Guindon. But, at the same time that he was struggling against the notion of a return to the past, there is no doubt whatever that, inwardly, he was wishing quite strongly that this all might really be happening.

It is difficult to determine what exactly was most involved in what Luc interpreted as a gap in time; was it the unbridled will of History? The disappointments of his own time or Luc's unrestrained desire to trace down his ancestral idol? Or quite simply, was it the methodical vagaries of his madness?

Whatever be the case, he had to face the facts: the carriages were still rattling along through the rainy night. A few ladies, as well, in nipped-in blouses and laced boots, with their skirts dragging in pools of water, were sauntering down rue Saint-Denis laughing beneath their umbrellas. Three men in bowler hats strode along behind them, stirred by the fragrance of damp skirts.

The bookseller couldn't help noticing Luc's pallor and haggard looks and he offered to bring the books to his home.

"I'll send someone for the money within a few days, if you find that suitable."

Luc neither agreed nor disagreed. He was ready to accept anything provided he was allowed to go outside for some fresh air and to cool off in that sluggish heavy shower ... This he did as soon as the bookseller had politely opened the door for him with a broad gracious gesture which evidently meant "So long for now, my dear friend."

Outside, Luc let the wind and rain penetrate his pores and his face, enjoying their invigorating effects, quite sure that the elements couldn't conceivably deceive him. He automatically headed towards the cafés; but once again, the logic of History brought him back to the realities of this other century; indeed, in that era when rue Saint-Denis served as sleeping quarters for the French-speaking shop-keeper class, he couldn't expect to find cafés there. The proof of this was hitting him with more and more force while growing broader in its scope. He took it all therefore as an accomplished fact. Was he not, on the other hand, the kind of man who preferred taking his desires for reality rather than reality for his desires?

While reflecting on this, he felt he was now fully integrated into that time period, though he still held fast to his awareness of the century of the atom, electron and skyscraper.

So he walked slowly along, going for a while down Saint-Denis, turning off onto Maisonneuve (or rather Mignonne), marching around the steeple of the Church of Saint-Jacques, then going back up Saint-Denis between the church and square of the same name; or else, he would walk down Ontario, returning along Sherbrooke, past the convent of the Sisters of the Good Shepherd, before going back up Saint-Denis while skirting the Bishop's Palace. And, in the very depths of his anguish, fearing then the night, the rain and the thunder, just as primitive man might have wondered as well how he was to survive in this unknown world where he had neither a haven nor any rightful place, Luc had the idea of going to the home of his memorable ancestor to seek asylum, protection ... and above all things, friendship. In 1878, Lucien Guindon was living just to the north of Courville, that is to say, today's Prince Arthur.

RUE ST-DENIS

Luc headed off then in the direction of that house that he had passed by hundreds of times without ever going in. To do this, he had turned off at Albina, walking beside the old la Côte à Barron reservoir, also called the Saint-Jean Baptiste reservoir, this green watery space which was to become public the following year and be named Saint-Louis Square two years later. While strolling by this old reservoir, among two anaemic street lamps and the impressive square of trees surrounding the basin and its fountain, still overwhelmed by the storm as the sun, rising behind thick clouds, slowly erased his shadow, it came to him that he would have to convince his grandfather that the time that separated them had just been nullified — that he, Luc, the son of a son still to be born some fifteen years later, who would be called Armand, was arriving there at the dawning of this day to ask him to embrace the impossible. But who better than this great mind, at the beginning of a fantastic career as a visionary, could greet this witness to the future without having him revert to a mad impossible world? What is more, it was perhaps this, Luc's arrival, that was the "momentous secret" which had given — or which was about to give — the deciding impetus to Lucien Guindon's career.

While the rain could be heard trickling over the leaves and tinkling like so many notes on the water's surface, Luc was thinking of all the material, all the information he could deliver to Lucien Guindon, of the role he could play in the elaboration of his great works. Perhaps he would be able to offer the world an immense cry of alarm and so protect some from the irresistible forces of the elements and others from disasters invented and propagated by man! Maybe he would be able to protect humanity from itself!

Luc then crossed Laval Street and walked along between the magnificent properties of Joseph Comte and Patrick Lawler, that is to say in little Courville Street. But far from encountering the numerous shops, the countless restaurants and murals of his own time, Luc discovered here in the dark the snug properties of the hustling and bustling shopkeeper class of that time. So he crossed both Cadieux and Sainte-Hyppolyte Street before going back up Saint-Dominique as far as the former rooming house of Lucien Guindon. When he was only a few steps from the house, the lighting inside cast a sort of shadow show of a fat woman standing in the wide entrance way; slightly behind her, as well, a bearded man seemed to be looking over her shoulder. No doubt, both of them were watching Luc as he came along in the rain, waving at him wildly to get inside as fast as possible. Luc did this without the slightest hesitation.

On the landing, he recognized the red-haired bookseller who, quite alarmed, scolded him for risking pneumonia or even toying with suicide by dawdling about like that in a rain storm.

"Look here, I left the bookstore a good couple of hours after your departure and I still arrived two hours before you did at your apartment! Your landlady, Madam Brisebois, and I were very worried ... "

"My apartment," Luc broke in!

Next, it was the landlady who administered the fatal blow.

"Tell us, Mister Lucien, do you feel all right? Come in and get dried out ... "

And while the stout woman and the bookseller were both engrossed in their anxiety over the sniffling young man, Luc ... or rather, Lucien, thought that there would be no one but himself to offer advice about his life's work and that all of it would be a waste of time since he already knew the contents of his future: "widespread derision and the hatefulness of ridicule," oblivion, then recognition ...

A recognition long delayed ...

CHRONOLOGY

1947 Birth at Hochelaga (Montreal) on October 21. Youth spent at Rosemont.

1960-1966 Louis-Hébert High School.
1966-1970 Bachelor of Pedagogy at Ville-Marie Normal School.
1970-1971 Bachelor of Arts (literary studies) at the University of Quebec at Montreal 1971-1973 Master of Arts (literary studies) UQAM.
1973-1975 Grant from the Quebec Ministry of Cultural Affairs (research on the independent press). Grant from the French government. Grant from the Canadian Arts Council. Courses towards a doctorate in psychology (semiology and gestaltism), Louis-Pasteur University (France).
1975-1980 Assistant director of the International Pavilion of Humour at Man and his World. Co-organizer of the Exhibit on the Quebec comic strip (1902-1976) at the Montreal Museum of Contemporary Art. Co-organizer of the exhibit of the Canadian comic strip shown in Europe.
1980-1983 Lecturer at UQAM and at the University of Montreal and reader for publishing houses. Grant from the Arts Council (support for creative writing). Co-organizer of the Boréal Congress on the fantastic and on science-fiction at the Montreal Book Salon (1983). Creation, research and animation of about forty literary broadcasts for Radio-Canada (1980-1983). 1983-1988 Literary columnist at *Littérature au pluriel, la Ronde des livres, Les Livres du jeudi, En toutes lettres* (1982-1984) Member of the jury for the Robert Cliche prize (1984). Co-founder of the grand Prix (Logidisque) for science-fiction and the fantastic in Quebec,

assuming the role of president from 1984-1986. Director of the collection "Dix Nouvelles" for the Quinze editions (1983-1987). Founding member of the review *XYZ, La revue de la nouvelle* (1985). Co-organizer, with Jacques Samson, of the first Round Table on the comic strip in Montreal at UQAM (1986). Member of the jury for the Humanitas prize and for the short story competition of the UQAM Module on literary studies (1986). Member of the jury for the Support Programme for Periodicals of the Quebec Ministry of Cultural Affairs (1986-1987). Member of the jury for the short story competition of the review *Vidéo-Presse*. Part-time professor for UQAM's Department of Literary Studies (1986-1987). Creator and animator for the broadcast, *Littératures parallèles*, on fantastic literature, science fiction, the detective novel and cartoon comics for the Radio-Canada FM network (1987-1988). Doctorate in French Studies, Sherbrooke University. Thesis on creative writing entitled "Diary of a Thousand Days. (Writing Diary). Diaristic essay" (1987). Director of the collection with XYZ editions (1987). Co-director since 1987, with Noël Audet, of the research group in literary creation at UQAM. Professor in the theory of literary creation for the Department of Literary Studies at UQAM.